Love by George

Robert Taylor

BLACK ROSE
writing™

ISBN: 978-1-61296-346-4

PUBLISHED BY BLACK ROSE WRITING

www.blackrosewriting.com

Printed in the United States of America

Love by George is printed in Plantagent Cherokee

To Sam, Maddie and Mary with love.

Love by George

"Someday, after mastering the winds, the waves, the tides and gravity, we shall harness for God the energies of love, and then, for a second time in the history of the world, man will have discovered fire." ~ Pierre Teilhard de Chardin

To someday!

Chapter 1

Aching, near breaking and long overdue,
in line, doin' time for uber-cuppa' joe;
Half-caf jones-in', fruity fiber scones-in',
bustin' out plastic, freakin' out, spastic;
In sighs, in butterflies, in bloodshot eyes,
we stand, we text, we wait... for what?
Another shot or two of get me thru –
no coffee, lunch or dinner date.

BLAH!

In a tangled corner of Facebook, a photo that a "friend" captioned "*Hope is about to wet herself*" roused a frightful throng of suitors. Seconds after going viral, a dozen Mr. Wrongs – mostly from the Chicago area – reacted. *Who snapped that picture!?!* wondered Hope, tripping on the words "wet herself" beneath her image. Like words were even necessary! The photo from last week's informal high school gathering said it all: Hope clutching a tipping glass, splashing wine onto her chest, eyeballs bulging. *Yay me!* she now thought, frozen in her swivel chair, a finger hovering over the delete key. Curiosity prevented her from hitting it. She scrolled down, reading the list of business contacts, classmates and others that she hadn't intended to inspire. Two names leaped off the monitor, Geoffrey and Cal – both textbook examples of what to expect when you lower the bar and date the leftovers.

Geoffrey responded with *There's a pill for that, Hopey. Take two and ring me in the morning.*

"I'd rather swallow tapeworms," said Hope aloud. "Ring"

hatched thoughts of fingers, hands and regurgitations of the night she spent in his company.

Their date could not have started better. Geoffrey arrived in a leather-seated Lexus. He opened every door and flattered at every opening. "Sorry," said Hope when they both spoke at the same time at the box office counter. "Didn't mean to interrupt."

"Oh, you're quite the opposite of an interruption," Geoffrey replied, eyeing Hope's leopard-print scarf and tight jeans. He twinkled down on her 5-foot-nothing frame and added, "I assure you." She needed someone like him, someone a foot taller, to pull off leopard print in the Windy City's back alleys. Stiffness marked her movements. Nerves, he thought, the kind one expects on a first date – standing next to a relative stranger, shifting weight from one leg to another, seeking an anchor, smiling at everything, looking down or away when silences lingered, though not from disinterest. A tingle in the air between them suggested otherwise. He attempted to engage her further by critiquing movies he had recently seen.

The topic afforded Hope time to conduct a thorough assessment of his face, beginning with his chocolaty eyes. Kindness and intelligence filled them. And random flashes of wonder when the conversation took a pleasant turn, as though curiosity had sparked mental footnotes. His nose held no special charm. More Roman than Greek, its principle highlight was that it featured nostrils clear of anything requiring a Kleenex or a scissor. Beneath it, his bottom lip protruded. At first glance, she thought that it could stand to be ratcheted in a notch or two. But upon further review, she rather fancied it, imagining Geoffrey weaving his fingers between her brunette tresses and presenting her the lip. So juicy. So plump. There for the taking.

His black mane glistened with hair product as he dropped his head and thumbed through his wallet. He paid in cash, not plastic, thinning a beefy stack of bills. After purchasing two tickets, he led Hope to the concession stand. "Popcorn?"

"Only if you don't mind butter."

"I wouldn't consume it any other way," he said. "It's good here. Cooked in real coconut oil. Actually, tonight the movie might be better than the popcorn. The critics gushed over this film. Of course they usually have their thumbs way up where they don't belong."

Hope laughed, wanting more. But the coming attractions ended as soon as they found seats, instilling a silence in him. *A movie buff*, thought Hope, imagining more small talk, perhaps over late-night coffee. "Regale me with some more of that opposite of an interruption talk" she might say if his brown eyes sparkled just a little more.

Twenty minutes later, he leaned and whispered, "Sooo … Busy tomorrow?" A wave of minty freshness brushed her ear.

She sighed while answering. "Tomorrow is out. Sorry. Deadline."

"Don't tell me the planets are aligned against us."

"Not if they know what's good for them."

"Deadline, huh?" he said with a sideways glance. "Forgot to ask. What do you do?"

"I write …,"

His eyes returned to the screen.

"… mostly poetry," she finished. *Oh, I see. Now I'm the interruption.* Had he uttered a compelling "oh?" or even an acknowledging grunt, she might have bared her Tennyson soul right then and there. Instead, bursts of light from the movie screen illuminated his insensitive cheek. *Still, he has potential,* she thought, willing her mind to remain open. *Rembrandt could have done something with his profile, I suppose, even in this darkness. Start mixing oils and … what the …?* His ear! In the light bursts, it appeared to elongate, and a bramble of hair emerged from deep inside. The visual instantly killed Rembrandt and Tennyson and inspired nothing but thoughts of birthing his hairy, elfin children. "Not much poetry in your world, I suppose," she blurted, attempting to turn his head.

"You got that right," said Geoffrey, unmoved.

"What kind of doctor? Forgot to ask."

He turned, looked Hope in the eyes and submerged his hand into the shared tub of popcorn. "Proctologist."

"Lovely," whispered Hope, scrambling through her handbag for sanitizing wipes. "*Aaand* there went my appetite."

Two bites later, his buttery hand fumbled onto her lap, latched onto her fingers and squeezed. The unexpected contact with the instrument of his profession propelled her from her seat to the ladies room. Immediately, she hit speed dial. "Ick! Ick! Ick! He touched me," she screeched. "Right on the hand."

"Hand touching on a date?" said April, Hope's bestie. She heard the sound of running water and pictured Hope lathering and scrubbing herself raw. "That's bold!"

"Oh, shut up! You'd freak too after being groped by a proctologist."

"Groped now? He washes after work, doesn't he? Of course, most guys don't wash like they should." The moment's irony was not lost on April. From memory, she could recite Hope's waking dream of masculine piano hands – supple and un-calloused, intertwining fingers with her own as they strolled on a New England beach a stone's throw from a lighthouse. Hope had zero tolerance for girly hands, clammy hands or sandpaper hands. Until that moment, she had never contemplated proctologist hands.

"Hand holding should not induce vomit," Hope fired back. "He felt like the Grim Reaper, all bony and cold. You'd think a proctologist would have warm hands."

The experience, though nearly a year old, remained ripe. Geoffrey's half-inch-square profile picture now on her computer monitor would, no doubt, worm its way into her nightmares again. Even so, she found it more palatable than the one below it. That picture belonged to Calvin, whose hands did not "glove up" for a living. He responded to Hope's captioned photo with: *Wetting yourself now? Sounds like someone needs a little Cal time. There's a new bar and grill downtown. Shall we?*

"We most definitely shall not!" snapped Hope. Not two months ago, Cal had wined and dined her at a black-tie only restaurant near Lake Michigan. Like Geoffrey, he made a solid first impression, thanks entirely to his cut of suit. Was it tailored? An Armani? The question, though pressing, went unasked. Hope never attracted worthy suits. *Don't ask, don't tell*, she thought. If it wasn't an Armani, she didn't want to know.

Black in color, it was either altered or a fortuitous fit – a skinny suit, highlighting muscle in all the right places. In the restaurant's half-light, he could have passed as the inspiration for Rodin's "The Thinker" – the model himself – who, after mulling things over, suddenly recalled the whereabouts of an impeccable wardrobe and suited up.

"Try not to drool," said Cal when the waitress presented menus.

"'Scuse me?" asked Hope.

"Never mind." He held out a pack of chewing gum. "Want some?"

She declined. He shoved two sticks into his mouth – chomping and sloshing and drowning out the background tinkling of champagne flutes, intimate conversations and a therapeutic cello. By the time the waitress returned, Hope expected his next utterance to be a "moo." Instead, he ordered mahi-mahi.

"Fettuccini Alfredo for me and a side of …," said Hope.

"Alfredo?" interrupted Cal. "You don't want that. You'll have to spend an extra hour in the gym tomorrow burning that off. It's cream sauce. Pure fat. Might as well order lard. Besides, seafood is the specialty here, not noodles."

"Seriously? Mmm-kay. Let me break it down for you. I'm getting the Alfredo. I'll pay for it myself if I have to. I happen to like cream sauce. Closer to love, actually. And if it's dripping with fat here, I bet it's real yummy. And FYI: Seafood doesn't agree with me. So don't go there. Not pretty."

Silence followed – relative silence – until Cal retired his

gum wad several minutes later. His eyes wandered until he thought to top off her water glass. Pouring, he risked a glance. "Nice place," he said weakly.

She glared back.

He looked away.

The tomato basil soup arrived. Hope turned it back and forth in her spoon, approving of its pulpy consistency. Its mix of cream, spice and tomato warmed her all the way down. *How much fat in a bowlful of epic crow?* she mused. *Can I get you a bowl of that, Cal?*

Entrees followed. Hope ate two of the three dinner rolls, mopping up Alfredo sauce from her plate. She asked the waitress for another basket. Bluffing indifference, Cal witnessed the ingestion of fat in horror.

Then came dessert.

"Whoa! Look at that," said Cal, ogling her tiramisu. "Mind if I …." Without consent, he took a bite. Before Hope could say, "Try that again and you'll pull back a bloody stump," his fork returned. And by his third bite, she had nothing more to say to him. Ever.

And yet, there his name appeared again, right on her computer, suggesting another calorie-counting adventure. *Rrright*, she thought. *Some faces need to go away.* She deleted his comment, then grabbed her handbag and scurried out the door.

Twenty minutes later, she stood second in line at a Lincoln Avenue coffee shop, still attempting to purge her thoughts.

"How *are* you?" the cashier asked the boxer-baring "boy" in front of her.

"Perfect." He dug into the recesses of his pants and produced a handful of coins. "I'll be even better after a green tea frapp."

"Perfect?" repeated the cashier. "From drinking mulch?"

Hope smirked. The rest of the line, like 21st century humanity at large, texted and Bluetooth-ed away, unhearing. *Sad,* she thought. *So much life happening. So many missing it.* It dispirited, yet inspired her. She reached for the pen and notebook in her handbag and jotted down "missing life – so much, so many." A downdraft of cologne awakened her senses further.

She turned and received its wearer eyes first, as was her habit at least once a week when *he* happened to be in the coffee line. Oh the smell of him! And the sight. And the rush she felt from his attention. The flutter was immediate, and she began the mental countdown:

Crooked smile (one thousand one, one thousand two), she thought. *Green eye twinkle (one thousand three), the nod (one thousand four) and POOF! Swallowed whole by his digital device. Gone in 5 seconds. Why can't a face like THAT appear on my Facebook page? I never attract faces like that. I can't even compete with his stupid smart phone. Just forget his face. He's already forgotten yours. Refocus. I need to be brilliant soon.*

Hope's phone rang, an all-too-familiar ringtone. *Why did I ever give her my number?* She shoved the notebook into her handbag. "About time you called. What's it been, an hour?"

"Great news, honey!" said her mother. "I got you a plot."

"A plot?"

"You know, at the cemetery. They had a buy-one-get-one-free deal. I bought a plot for you and your future husband, that is, *if* you ever find one."

"Geez, Mom! Could you be any weirder? Look, I need to focus on my job interview *not* my rotting corpse!"

The outburst jolted the coffee line. En masse, they looked up, unnaturally stirred from the digital world. Hope froze – everything but her fingers. Instinctively, they fumbled through her handbag.

"Yoo hoo?" said her mother. "You there?"

Releasing a cigarette, Hope cupped her hand and lowered her voice. "Uh, barely. Did you plan my funeral too?"

"This is the gratitude I get? Typical. When's the interview?"

"Half an hour."

"Did you wear your hair up or down?"

"Up. Why?"

"You didn't read your horoscope today, did you? Should have worn it down. Up makes you look old."

"It's not too late for parenting classes, Mother. Look, I gotta' go." She hung up and shook her head.

"Rough day, toots?" asked the cashier.

"You have *nooo* idea. You'd think that putting your mother up for adoption would be easier than this. *Still* no takers."

The cashier chuckled. "The usual?"

"Please."

"You got it. Venti caramel macchiato with soy, no room, no fun."

"Story of my life," mumbled Hope, suddenly feeling the effects of denying herself whipped cream – "fun" in coffee talk – and the growing list of life's little things. She checked her watch. Within the hour, she would try to convince Love by George, the third largest online dating company, that they needed a woman of her talents: a woman whom half of the baristas referred to as "High Maintenance Latte" and the rest simply called "No Fun."

Chapter 2

Had George Theodore Marble – "Ted" – Love by George CFO, lost himself in self-help books instead of *The Cheat St. Journal*, the day-to-day business of matchmaking would have induced fewer ulcers. Singlehandedly, Ted created milk of magnesia dependency. In a thunderous voice, he addressed office fires large and small. "I'm your boss, not your therapist!" he barked, or, "Don't you have something to do other than waste my time?"

Even in silence, he encroached upon his surroundings. It was his constant scowl. It was the way he belted and projected his belly like a weapon. The way he cracked his knuckles when words failed. His fingernails clipped to the nubs. His militant flattop and pencil-thin moustache that danced when agitated.

The recent stock market slide only worsened his disposition. His minions swapped who-peed-in-his-Cheerios-today theories and hallway dares to call him "Marbles." Office morale suffered until the afternoon that Hope dropped off her resume package. That day, the Dow swelled 400 points. A kinder, gentler Ted – the rarest of creatures – emerged from his corner office sounding like the Dalai Lama.

Mid-morning, he chided his secretary – whose diet embraced sugar and fat in stunted portions – with, "Life's too short for half a donut, Mary." At noon, after a powwow with his broker, he treated employees to pizza. "It's only money," he said when thanked. And by the Dow's closing bell, that afternoon, he smiled without condescension.

Only Liz, the office mouthpiece, had the guts to test his mood. "Niiice," she said, pointing to his socks. "Is that a cry for help?"

“My socks?” asked Ted. “What’s wrong with them?”

“Isn’t it obvious? Socks 101: Always wear black socks with black shoes unless your socks match your pant color perfectly. On second thought, scratch that. Just stick with black. Matching isn’t your thing, peacock.” This set the minions buzzing – all female, all attired in blacks and grays, all releasing pent-up critique.

“What are you talking about?” asked Ted, his eyes narrowing. “I match. My pants and socks *are* green.”

“Someone needs his eyes checked.”

Even at this, Ted’s mood held, until someone uttered the phrase “ankles crying for help.”

“So let me get this straight, Liz,” sneered Ted. “Next time I hit the men’s store, I should bring my entire sock collection and hold them up to every *freaking pair* of slacks before making a purchase?”

At precisely that moment, Hope walked through the front door.

Spinning around, Ted said, “And what’s *your* take?” He lifted a pant leg.

“My take?” asked Hope. “On your socks?”

He nodded.

“Not bad, although, hmmm.”

“Hmmm what?”

“Well, it’s just … I might have gone with black.”

Ted’s eyes bulged. “I might have gone with black,” he flouted in a girly voice, then stomped down the hallway.

“Sorry!” Hope called out after him. “Just trying to help.”

Three weeks later, fresh off her no-fun coffee run, Hope returned for her interview. In the interim, she had submitted a dozen applications across the metro area, whispering a prayer with each one. Love by George was the only response.

And so, for the second time that month, she paused outside the building. Closing her eyes, she absorbed the downtown Chicago vibe: the multi-lingual chatter, the honking taxis, the whining brakes, the flutters of wind stirring the urban potpourri. *Time to stand out,* she thought. *Time to make an impression. Now picture calling this place the office.* Drawing a deep breath, she exhaled and glanced up. Completed half a century ago, The John Hancock Center stood resolute – 100 stories of aluminum, concrete and glass, head and shoulders above its surroundings. Black support beams zigzagged up the facade, pointing skyward, leaving impressions of movement and purpose. She thought about how disappointed the architect must be that everyone called it "The Cock." If anything, it appeared inspired by argyle. *Hey, maybe I'll bump into the sock guy again. Now there's someone who knows how to stand out!* She threaded through the ambulating crowd and pushed the rotating door.

Ewww, she thought, stopping at the elevator, eyeing the yellowed button panel. *Wouldn't catch me touching those.* But someone had to. The attendant, a Mr. Chester "Mac" MaGillicutty – according to his name badge – clearly deserved a raise. He maintained the air of one who braved such perils with neither fear nor sanitizing wipes.

"Where to then, ma'am?" he asked.

"37th floor please."

"Love by George, aye?" Mac pressed button 37. "Ever been t'the top?"

A coffee stain prevented her from reply. *Ugh! Why did I wear a white shirt?* She found a tissue in her handbag and feverishly dabbed inward on her chest.

Mac handled the crisis like a trained professional. He executed a Marine-style about face as the doors closed. Several decades of tips taught him that respecting a passenger's dignity was a solid financial move.

The ascent should have been a cinch for Hope – some minor bracing, focused breathing, channeling all thought elsewhere – usually to the mountains or the sea. Controlling this breath, the next and another, she found her oxygen on elevators. But absorbed as she was with dabbing, she neglected her coping mechanisms. Between the 15^(th) and 16^(th) floor, her knees buckled. Vertigo and wheezing followed.

When the elevator stopped and the doors opened, Mac tipped his cap and attended to her teetering state. "Steady there," he said, catching her by the elbow. "Thirty-seventh floor. Off ye go now, *care*-fully."

Hope remained outside the doors until the world stopped spinning. She grabbed her phone and opened a text from April: *dazzle time, no?* it read. *as n intervu? both barrels, girl! don't 4get fado's 2nite. will mop up what's left of u.*

crossing my fingers. not holding my breath, apes, Hope replied, as she felt her lungs fill again.

Karli, the Love by George receptionist, received her at the front desk with an apology. "The interviews are running long today," she said, with pleasantness that sounded rehearsed. "Please make yourself comfortable. You look like you need to sit down. Mary will come in a few minutes."

Hope found a stiff polka dot chair and flitted through a magazine. *Why am I here?* she wondered as the minutes ticked by. *What do I know about online dating? What happened to chasing my dream? To owning my own coffee shop? I should be there right now – sipping lattes, cranking out poems, sitting in a chair that makes my butt happy.* She crossed her legs back and forth and sensed Karli's eyes upon her.

Hope's gaze drifted to the cream-colored walls and the framed pictures of abandoned beaches. *I'd give anything to be there. How long has it been since my toes touched sand? If only.* She sighed, recalling a poem that she had penned in college – when her brain was still washed in saccharine – about chasing life's *if onlys.* How did life lead her here? Jaded by reality, she grabbed her notebook and captured the moment:

> *In fits and fidgets, in fractures and frights,*
> *the hot seat whelps a flustered bowel.*

Half-a-Donut Mary finally appeared. "Sorry to keep you

waiting," she percolated. "You ready?"

Hope stood and nodded. *Define ready. Something tells me you've never had a flustered anything.* She followed Mary down a corridor adorned with photos of successfully matched couples, all smug and glowing, almost surreal. Were they actors? One couldn't help but wonder. Mary stopped at the corner office. She knocked and opened the door, then quickly excused herself. Inside, in front of the far wall, from behind a mahogany desk, Ted paced back and forth. *Sock guy?* thought Hope, gasping. *He's my interview?*

"Cripes!" he barked into his cell phone. "Just how many Bobs are there in New Delhi? Here's the scoop, Bob. I drive a Mercedes. Your monthly salary there wouldn't cover an oil change. Try pushing used car warranties somewhere else." He folded up his phone and tossed it onto his desk. "The English language deserves better treatment than that," he mumbled before glancing at Hope. "You again, the fashion expert." He picked up his coffee mug and sipped.

"Had I known the socks were such a delicate matter," said Hope as Ted motioned for her to sit. "I never would have ...,"

"Forget it," he interrupted, picking up her file. "Hope, uh, Allday. Allday? Really? First India Bob, now this. What are the odds? Can I get you coffee?"

"No thanks. I just had some."

"I see that. Kind of jumps right off your shirt."

"Couldn't help but notice the name on your door," said Hope, redirecting. "Mr. George Marble, is it?"

"I'm not *that* George if that's what you're getting at. Not the company namesake. Don't you watch TV? I thought everyone knew George's face. *That* George leaves the interviews to me. I go by Ted here." He opened her file and read, periodically glancing over his reading glasses. Email alerts on his computer beeped without pause. Sock guy was important. His tone implied that, a tone that sounded accustomed to giving orders.

She gleaned what she could from his decor: a swordfish, a Harvard diploma and two framed slogans: "Check yourself at the door" and "Imagine you, only better." *Well, this guy just pukes sunshine,* she thought, her eyes drifting to the wall of windows behind him. She imagined standing there, conducting business over the phone, towering over the downtown below.

"Not much corporate experience," said Ted finally, setting down her file.

"Just the job right out of college."

He smirked. "Yeah, I caught that. The stint with Oprah. I'd be lying if I said I weren't curious: You earn a marine biology degree from the University of Tampa, relocate to Chicago – hundreds of miles from either ocean – then find Oprah. And wind up peddling Hallmark cards. How exactly does that happen?"

Hope did not blink. "Okay. I'll just be blunt. If life were a dot-to-dot, I'd have a pretty righteous scribble going about now. Then again, who doesn't? I like poetry better than biology and television. It just took me a while to figure that out. I followed the adage on your wall: I imagined myself, only better. And I don't work for Hallmark. I make my own greeting cards."

"Bust-out-the-Kleenex stuff I hear."

"Excuse me? My customers say …,"

"The country club just confirmed," Mary's voice suddenly blared over the intercom. "4:15 tee time."

"4:15, huh?" repeated Ted, pushing a button and speaking into the microphone. "That works. Take the afternoon off, Mary. I'm just wrapping things up here." He picked up his cell phone, dialed a number and held an index finger up at Hope. "Just a minute," he mouthed, then swiveled his chair and gazed out the windows. "Al? Yeah. Ted here. 4:15 is a go. Better bring your wad of cash. Last time was a fluke. I've been practicing."

"… my customers say," whispered Hope, "that my cards are full of heart." She nearly stood and walked out. The jostling in her chair was sufficient enough to hike her panties upward. *I can't sit here like this,* she thought. Gripping the armrests with both hands, she inched backward, attempting to right herself.

Ted swiveled back. He raised a brow and picked up her file again. "Barry Manilow?" he said. "The wonders never cease.

Dude falls in love five seconds into every song. Sooo unnatural. And getting hit up for a date at the unemployment office. Another one of your Hallmark moments."

"What?" huffed Hope. "How did you …?" *I didn't put anything about Barry Manilow or the unemployment office on my application.*

"Doesn't matter how. It's good reading material." He waved a dismissive hand. Hope's eyes blazed back at him. "Oh very well, then. If you *must* know." He picked up the phone and hit a button. "Mary? Hope's background: Where did you dig that up?"

Hope leaned forward, straining to hear. "Facebook," he announced, hanging up. "The How-Well-Do-You-Know-Hope Allday Quiz. Public information, I am told. Hard to believe what people disclose online about their personal lives these days. Marvelous tool, the internet."

"What?!?" fumed Hope. "You can't do that."

"Can! And did!"

Hope shot up from her chair. "We are sooo finished here."

"Sooo soon? What about the why-should-we-hire-you question? It's my favorite."

Hope's eyes narrowed. "Right after you answer the how-good-is-your-lawyer question."

"Ah well, fine, if you want to get ugly about it. We have an attorney on staff, you know. He's good. Very good. But so is your timing. I'm off to strike golf balls now. Maybe I'll buy some socks along the way. Black, not green if memory serves." He referenced her file one last time. "Oh, by the way, I too enjoy a good bubble bath."

From the elevator, Hope rummaged through her handbag, finding a cigarette, her last, the same one that she had fondled an hour ago in the coffee shop. The emergency cigarette. She had quit smoking a month ago. Cold turkey. Until now. *Where is Mac?* she wondered, riding down the elevator alone. *Why isn't he here to stop me?* She lit up, took a drag and patted down her coat pockets. *OMG! My cell phone. I must have left it.* She punched the button panel until the elevator stopped, too full of rage to feel germs. She crushed the cigarette with her stiletto and braced for the ride back up. With salvaged dignity, she burst through the Love by George front door, found her phone on the polka-dot chair and turned to leave.

"Well, well, well. Look who's ...," chided Ted from the front desk. Then he pointed at her chest. "Look, everyone! This girl really *is* on fire! Sing it with me now ...."

"Huh?" A thin bead of smoke curled up from Hope's cleavage. Concealing her fright, she flicked a smoldering ash at Ted. "Here's a little souvenir for you to remember me by."

"Don't think I need one, sweetheart. Not after that impression."

"How did *you* wind up in the love industry? I'd be lying if I said that *I weren't curious.* You're the one who needs to go imagine yourself better. I can't. You're not even human, you ...," stammered Hope, "you ... sock Neanderthal!"

As she stormed out, the commotion extracted the other George – Mr. Love-by-George himself – from his office.

"You just missed the show," said Ted.

"Good interview?" asked George.

"Smokin!"

Chapter 3

Time had no hold on April. Her battery of excuses for tardiness rivaled none: Lost my pen – forgot I tucked it in my ear (15 minutes late). Couldn't find my car in the parking lot (30 minutes late). Stuck in the toilet. Really (an hour late). That time, her boyfriend had left the seat up. When she sat down, her derriere plunged into the water. Wriggling her hips from beneath the toilet lip was no small task. When she finally escaped, she had to bathe again. At least once a year, she blamed delays on the time change, but even when falling back an hour, she found a way to be late. "There will always be un-knowables," she explained when made to feel guilty, "and I can't tell you what they will be."

Today, a trip to the pet store delayed her. Vinny, her boa constrictor, had gone without his dietary staple for two days – something she nearly forgot to buy after seeing the Westie puppies (today's un-knowable). She lost half an hour cuddling them and cooing. Then the sky opened with a clap of thunder. The deluge slowed traffic and sent the mercury plummeting 20 degrees. That's why she entered Fado's Irish Pub an hour past the appointed time. Wiping her feet, she retracted her umbrella and raked fingers through her hair. *Odd,* she thought, looking about, not seeing Hope. *It's after 5 o'clock. Did she say 6?*

"Welcome to Fado's!" the hostess shouted over Celtic music. She eyed April, wondering why anyone would wear sunglasses in the dark. "How many in your party?"

"Just two." April craned to see past her. A suspended rope ladder twisted down from the ceiling. It terminated at a distant staircase. The ladder bisected the dining area, highlighting the room's two main features: a praying monk portrait beneath the ceiling to the right, and, to the left, a pristine sail bearing the name "fado." The sail hung from a support beam and partially concealed the upstairs seating. Everything else was wooden – floors, tables, chairs, the walls. April felt like she had boarded an ancient vessel. She contemplated the praying monk. Would he bless or curse such a voyage? The ebb and flow of laughter and wafts of sweet ale suggested anything but a curse.

"This way please." The hostess led April to an upstairs table. She presented a drink menu and wondered again at the sunglasses. "Your waiter should be here shortly."

i'm here. where r u? April texted Hope. She then extracted the evening's accoutrements from her handbag and arranged them like place settings: a notebook, two pens and a Wite-Out roller. *Will Hope's feng shui eye approve?* she wondered. She repositioned the shorter pen, moving it further away from the notebook. The exercise, like so much about her friend, amused her.

Hope, a functioning OCD, chased her dreams by day, then second-guessed them when her head hit the pillow. Nothing was perfect. Everything could always be better. Bending life to her will, she accepted nothing as-is. Except people. In people, even the ordinary, Hope found worth, not fault. Friends like Hope, April knew, could be counted on a single hand. Real friends. Friends that buy you Gucci handbags when you are not Gucci material. Before Hope, April thought herself only worthy of knockoff brands and cheap beer. Now, she eyed the Guinness two tables over with a sense of anticipation.

April pointed to the dark brew when the waiter arrived. "How about two of those thingees?"

"Build yer a perfect pint then?" he asked.

"You build drinks here?"

"Aye," said the waiter. "Op'n the tap, fill yer glass up halfwise. Wait fer the foam tuh settle. Add a second layer. Put a lil heart in the foam if ye' like. Popular wi the laydees. Hundred nineteen seconds tuh build a perfect pint from scratch."

"Perfection in less than two minutes? Sold! One for me and one for my imaginary friend."

The waiter nodded, taking down the order. "Brilliant! By the by, yer vibratin' some'n' fierce."

April cocked her head. "Sorry?"

The waiter brushed his sleeve, flashing a veiny bicep, then pointed to her phone with his pen. "Yer mo-bile," he said. "Vibratin' like a blue-arsed fly."

"Oh. I best get that."

speeding ticket. eyelash batting = epic fail, Hope texted. Ten minutes later, she finally arrived, just as the waiter returned. He placed two sudsy tulip-shaped glasses on coasters. "How goes it t'day?" he asked Hope.

"Like the second voyage of the Titanic," she answered.

"Per'aps some bangers and mash, then. If that don't right the ship, nothin' will. It's t'day's special."

"Sounds like a plateful of violence."

"Nay," he answered. "'Tis aye-rish pork sausage on col-cannon with … Holy Mary and Martha!" He took a step backward and stared at April. She had removed her sunglasses to read the menu and uncovered a black eye that jumped right off her ivory skin. "What the …?"

Hope squared her shoulders. "Never seen a female boxer before, love?"

"A boxer?"

Suddenly, the bar stool crowd erupted. Swaying arm in arm, they raised steins and toasted the latest English football goal in song: a melodic stream of "oles" and "oooles" in tight repetition.

"Violence it is!" shouted Hope over the ruckus. "One order. Two plates. The faster, the better!"

The waiter nodded then retreated to the kitchen.

April clasped Hope's forearm. "Thanks," she said. Few accepted her black eye explanations. Everyone assumed that a boyfriend beat her. It wasn't true. Neither was the boxing. The truth was a harder sell: sleepwalking. Last night, it happened again. April had disassembled her bed frame and used the boards to build a corral for an imaginary horse. In doing so, she slipped, banged her head then awakened.

Her nocturnal activities no longer panicked her as they did when they first manifested in late adolescence. She raised doctors' eyebrows by scoring a 13 on the Epworth Sleepiness Scale (zero through nine is considered normal). A battery of sleeping tests followed. With Frankenstein wires, specialists monitored her brain waves, heart rate and respiration. Screened her for common fatigue, anxiety and panic attacks. Checked her drug and alcohol levels. Then tested for personality disorders. In the end, doctors eliminated everything but sleepwalking, a rarity among adults. There was no preventing it. No pills to curb it. No therapeutic cure. There was nothing to do but accept it, something April did in her early 20s. Still, given the choice, she preferred not to discuss it, especially with strangers. She treasured Hope for heading off inquiries. "It looks worse than it feels," said April, putting on her sunglasses again. "It sounds like your day was worse than my night."

"Not at first glance," replied Hope. "I'll fill you in later. Let's just get this over with." Hope opened her Dream Notebook and flipped to the latest entry. Try as she might, she could not fathom how cyberspace found recreation in her dreams. But April needed them. She posted them with "anonymous" tags on her website after interpreting them.

Tonight's dream would become *Anonymous 30-Something Installment #26.* The previous 25 had created something of a stir. Who was Anonymous 30-Something? Dream interpretation junkies wanted to know. April would not reveal Hope's identity, so followers learned what they could from each installment and swapped analyses theories using the site's chat boxes. Hope thought the whole business to be absurd. But that was the deal: her dreams for April's words and phrases. They met once a month for the exchange.

"In this dream, I was in D.C.," began Hope, "and *he* was there."

"Headless again?" asked April.

"No. Fully capitated this time, only with blue eyes. No other discernible features."

April's pen stopped writing. "Blue? What happened to green? Maybe Mr. Yum Yum at the coffee shop isn't worth your five seconds after all."

"Probably not. Yesterday, I decided that he peddles urinal cakes for a living and douses himself in cologne to cover the odor. That way I can write him off before he lets me down. Anyway, back to the dream, *Blue Eyes* was working at an information booth, translating Dutch poetry into English. I was walking past his booth when I heard his voice and stopped. I was on my way to – How in the world do you keep a straight face while I tell you this? – on my way to a tulip festival. Our eyes met. Then, feeling something cold on my feet, I looked down. The streets were flooded with water. It was teeming with strange fish. Not real fish. They looked like metallic Picasso doodles."

"And then?" asked April.

"Then nothing. I woke up. No need to interpret this one. Allow me: Means I should be committed, right?"

"It means website hits. Floods are about tension. Something in your life needs to be released. *Love* the Picasso doodles and poetry. That's a nice twist. No idea what to make of it yet. I'll check the interpretation manuals. What a dream! You had a breakthrough: You looked into his eyes. That indicates an understanding. And that's not even the main event. The highlight is definitely the tulips. They usually suggest a new beginning. But this time, I think the alternate meaning applies. Since *he* – your recurring Mr. Perfect – looked you in the eyes, tulips more than likely means kissing. You know, two lips."

"Right!" said Hope. "Or it means he is to be admired, not plucked."

Further exploring the two lips angle, April talked plumpness, elasticity and technique. Hope just chugged beer and nodded, indulging her. April was a bad fit for corporate America. She couldn't show up at an employer's office looking like she did now. Fortunately, her dream interpretation website paid the bills – thanks to advertising dollars from sleeping pill manufacturers and mattress companies. But the website was more than a revenue stream. It allowed April to study dreams that were all safe and tucked in and didn't leave her bruised.

Several minutes later, April shared her words and phrases: innocuous, share-worthy, dancing with the psychos, ice cream intervention and a few others.

"Ice cream intervention," repeated Hope in contemplation. "Where'd that come from?"

"Oh, that's all mine, I'm afraid. I'm on my third pint of Ben & Jerry's Raspberry Peach Cobbler. It's a limited edition flavor. It needs to go away. Eleven grams of fat per serving. It's a dress size or two every time I open the freezer."

Hope jotted it down with the same anticipation she had two years ago after hearing April's word "impetuity." Toying with it, Hope had come up with "somewhere between the heart's impetuity and the mind's reserve" – the money phrase in her best-selling Valentine's Day card. "Ice cream intervention," Hope said again. "That's good."

"What about you? Any new poems?"

"Nothing share-worthy. Gonna' tell me about that shiner now or should I guess?"

After taking a long draught of her Guinness, April shared what she remembered of the imaginary horse and the night before. "My eye looks better now than it did this morning," she said. "I iced it for an hour." She grabbed Hope's notebook, flipped to the latest poem and read it aloud:

In fits and fidgets, fractures and frights,
the hot seat whelps a flustered bowel;

In vacant stares, in un-swiveled chairs,
in no mistaking no one cares;
In plastic smiles, it hits the fan
with no one really looking –
that fateful day that someday dies,
shattering dreams in last reprise.

"No death talk here, mum, if ye pleez," said the waiter, reappearing. "Just a wee bit sooper-stee-shus, I yum." He placed the bangers, mash and an extra plate on the table, then tripped over April's handbag – launching its contents, including the vacuum-sealed 10-pack of Vinny's frozen rats, across the hardwood floor. Surrounding tables gasped, drowning out the buzz from the football match.

"Oh! My! Gosh!" screeched Hope. She dropped to the floor and helped April refill her bag with lipsticks and eyeliners. "You are *not* putting that back in here," she said, pointing to the rat pack.

When they returned to their seats, Hope lectured. "Vermin have *no* place in a Gucci handbag!" she fumed. "Rats and leather: bad combination!" On and on she went, sounding more than a little bit like her mother, talking about all that is good and right and sacred in the world. In conclusion, she referenced an Aldo Gucci quote: "The bitterness of poor quality is remembered long after the sweetness of low price has faded from memory."

With the rats now on her lap, April calmly replied, "It just didn't feel right leaving Vinny's rats in the car, out there in the rain and cold. He prefers them at room temperature."

Laughter followed, the kind that leaves you in tears.

They ordered a second round of Guinness, and Hope rehashed the day's interview, now able to find humor in it. The clock struck midnight before the friends parted ways.

Exhausted when she arrived home, Hope nestled beneath the covers and struggled with the voices in her head: Voices accusing her of wasting a decade chasing greeting card dreams. Voices saying that she deserved Ted's abuse. That Mr. Right didn't exist.

The prospect of never finding *him* induced the sharpest pain. By day, her job search distracted from thoughts of *him,* whoever he was. She didn't need *him*, she told herself, friends, family. After all, her brain dictated her fate, not her heart. But at night, in bed alone, there was no denying what bubbled up – something she couldn't shake, a whisper that she was only half-alive.

Chapter 4

The pre-dawn, West Virginian fog meant one thing to the convenience store clerk: belligerent tourists. Today, they would not be whining about the price of gasoline. "Looks like I won't be taking *any* pictures this morning!" they would bemoan instead, like he had something to do with it. Browsing through the display rack of Spruce Knob and Seneca Rocks postcards would further antagonize them.

"It'll lift," he would reply with a look of knowing. "That's the kind of fog that burns off before noon." He had pacified their kind before with these words, pretending to care. It was part of the 5:00 a.m. routine: birds chirped, coffee percolated and national recreation area tourists facing less than perfect weather soured. Didn't matter. Everything was done. The shelves were stocked. The pastries aligned. The floor tiles bleached. Maybe only ten more customers in the next hour before he clocked out, and the pretending stopped. Tick tock.

At present, he stood behind the cash register and contemplated a solitary figure at the beverage station – hiking boots, cargo pants, a Columbia jacket, a ball cap pulled down low. He filled a coffee cup with Kona blend, no cream, no sugar. His name escaped the clerk. His face did not. He had seen this man before.

Suddenly, the front door opened, breaking the silence. A busload of retirees shuffled in – polyester-clad, whistling dentures, painted-on eyebrows. "Great," muttered the clerk. They would destroy his bathrooms, he knew, deplete his coffee creamers and ransack the condiments. Everything would need doing again.

Mr. Kona Blend sidestepped the parade. He stopped just short of the cash register when a blue hair said, "Not in *my* living room!" A mounted deer head on the wall appeared to sicken her.

The head was not for sale, but it roused her husband's recollection of a stuffed badger, stashed away in the garage back home. "*Forty* years of marriage," he grumbled, "and still not a *single* representation of my personality in my own home. What do you think of that, Mr. Buck? Makes me want to mark territory."

"Oh, you mark it every day, Fredrick," his wife shot back. "If you ever cleaned a toilet, you would know it. Fine! If it means that much to you, go ahead and mount that *nasty* rodent on the bathroom wall when we get home."

He scowled. "The bathroom?"

"You heard me. There's room over the toilet."

"The toilet?" Now Fredrick's bifocal-ed eyes danced. "What am I supposed to do? Barge in on company while they're doing their business? Sorry to interrupt, but hey, you're the first one to go eyeball to eyeball with my badger and hold a steady aim. Way to be! And it's a mustelid, not a rodent!"

"Mustelid? Oh that's rich! Good to know that all that time you spend reading on the can is finally paying off. And me here to witness it. What a lucky girl I am!"

"Five minutes, people!" the bus driver interjected. He positioned himself between the feuding couple and stretched out his arms. The twosome glared back at him and then each other before dispersing in opposite directions.

With nothing more to entertain him, Mr. Kona Blend stepped up to the cash register. He set down his cup on the counter and extracted a money clip from his front pocket.

"The light bulb just went off!" exclaimed the clerk. "You're the Love by George guy on TV: Mr. Compatibility Test. Ha! Took me a while to put the name to the face."

"Just a tourist today," said George. He put his finger to his mouth in a shushing gesture then laid a $50 bill on the counter. "And I'd like to keep it that way."

"Rrrrrright. Gotcha," said the clerk, pushing the money back. "But hey, you don't have to ..."

"Keep it." George picked up his cup and walked away.

"You sure? I mean. Thanks, man, but ..."

"Never been more sure of anything in my life."

"You ought to give folks an *incompatibility* test," called out the badger-man. "Cupid's aim sucks. Just ask the wife."

George hoisted his cup and flashed his TV smile, then opened the door and disappeared. *Mission accomplished,* he thought as he got in his SUV and drove off. *Got in, got coffee, got out. No autograph, no photographs. Only $50. A bargain.*

Through the windshield, he watched the darkness retreat in the Monongahela National Forest. The dim, pre-sunrise aura outlined clusters of hickory, oak, maple and spruce in a misty wake. He turned off the radio. Nature demanded silence at this hour. George listened. Cracking the window, he let in the potpourri of damp bark and leaves. *That smell,* he thought. *That quiet. It's a New England shiver. Like the Headless Horseman might appear angry and galloping.* For the next half hour, a luminous glow expanded across the horizon. He sipped coffee and rolled along in no particular hurry. It was his first visit here. Probably his last. But in that singular moment, George Springs III felt alive ... until his cell phone rang a few minutes later. *Forgot to turn that stupid thing off.* Answering it was out of the question.

Were he at the office, he would probably be in a meeting. Or in a meeting about a meeting. Or pulling slides together for his next meeting. Why? So someone could exercise words like ideation and functionality before scheduling yet another meeting. Since founding Love by George, he had attended exactly 528 meetings. He knew because he documented them all in a notebook: time, date, attendees, purpose, anything worth remembering. After 10 years of meetings, he had filled only two notebooks. Notebook number three would be his last, he promised himself.

Lately, he made only mandatory appearances. When meetings could not be avoided, he met on the golf course, which only tainted the golf. Too much talking between shots. Still, it beat being chained to a desk. And he had Ted for backup. Ted could handle most meetings without him. That's what was happening today: Ted was covering for him in Chicago.

For now, only George's GPS was privy to his whereabouts. "This should be short and sweet," he said to himself, rolling to a stop, killing the ignition. He recognized the ridge ahead from photographs. It tumbled sharply into the meadow below. His destination was close – Spruce Knob, the highest peak in the state. In less than 10 minutes, he would be there. He would canvas the ground for a golf-ball-sized rock – most likely sandstone – shove it into his coat pocket and cross West Virginia off his list. After that, only nine states would remain. Just nine more until he could claim to have scaled every state's summit and have the rock samples to prove it. He was saving Alaska's Mount McKinley – all 20,320 feet of it – for last. Spruce Knob was no Mount McKinley. It was 15,000 feet closer to sea level and only 900 feet from his car.

Taking a can of pepper spray and nothing else, George hiked out of the parking area. *Haven't needed this since hmmm ...?* he thought. He checked the expiration date on the can and remembered. *Montana.* He had company that day, Paige Walker, a budding *Chi-Town Trib* reporter.

A one-time Miss Illinois, Paige turned heads with her strawberry blonde hair, long legs and ambition. "I'm outdoorsy," she had assured George when they met, begging to tag along on his Montana excursion. "I can handle the climb." In return, she promised front-page coverage in the Sunday paper.

The PR was too good for George to pass up. They met before sunrise one Saturday on the outskirts of Yellowstone National Park. They planned to go "moosing" before scaling the 12,000-

foot peak in the Beartooth Mountains. George had offered to pick up Paige after moosing – to save her from the alarm clock, to let her sleep in and breakfast properly. "It is the weekend after all," he said.

"You're sweet," said Paige, "but I didn't come all this way for beauty rest. I'm here to make a few harmless observations. I'll stay out of the way. You'll hardly notice me." She required few details. She already had her angle: Mr. Compatibility – the toast of Chicago whom no one seemed to know a thing about – at play, trailblazing boldly into the woods. The story would write itself. Meanwhile, she could determine why there was no ring on his finger.

Shortly after entering the woods that morning, George halted and made a stop signal. "Look!"

"What?" asked Paige.

George inched forward and pointed. A porcupine clung to the base of a willow shrub, motionless, concealed in a cage of branches.

Squinting, Paige made out two black eyes, then the rest of its prickly frame. "He'll shoot! He'll shoot!" she cried.

"Porcupines don't shoot. They only stick you if you touch them."

In hysterics, Paige insisted that an aerial assault was imminent. George's calmness on the matter and the absence of flying quills eventually convinced her otherwise. *How stupid I must have sounded*, she thought. *And he laughed!* It was *her* job, not his, to expose ignorance. She was the reporter. But there was no saving face out there in the sticks. How was she to know that porcupines didn't shoot? *Didn't I see that on TV once?* Humiliated, she felt the urge to flee. "I'll just wait in the car," she said, turning away.

With a look of compassion, George grabbed her hand. He led her deeper into the willows, shielding her body with his as they passed the porcupine. They proceeded in silence for a quarter of an hour until two cow moose — each with a calf in tow —

emerged from the willows only 50 feet from where they stood. George crept forward, camera first, as one moose charged another.

"Pssst!" whispered Paige, tugging on George's jacket sleeve. "Take me back! *Now!*"

"This is a once-in-a-lifetime shot. Just stay behind me."

That's when the yipping began. It came from somewhere behind.

"Wolves, wolves!" yelled Paige.

"Coyotes, not wolves. That's yipping. Wolves don't yip. Besides, wolves would never ..."

Cowering, Paige screeched louder, "Wolves, wolves!"

This fresh wave of fright – hands shaking, her face deplete of color – was even more spectacular than the first. Again George laughed. Mortified, Paige bolted. "Those aren't ...," George called out after her, belly laughing. Her shoulder-length hair bobbed and swayed. She weaved through the willow patch in a full sprint back to the car. "They're not wolves!" he yelled.

Minutes later, George was driving Paige to the airport. She had fallen ill rather suddenly, she claimed – dizzy, cramping, something she ate, perhaps the elevation. Words were few during the commute, except for exchanged apologies that they both dismissed: She was sorry for ruining his adventure. He was sorry that he didn't escort her back to the car. He now detected a hint of raspberry lotion on her. *How did I miss that before?* he wondered. *Probably best that she's leaving. Not good to hit grizzly country smelling like a fruit snack.*

Later that afternoon, after Paige's plane touched down at O'Hare, she arrived at her urban safe house and found an upset tummy basket on her doorstep – club soda, crackers, peppermint, bananas and a greeting card. "To your health!" it read, with a raised champagne flute on the cover. Inside, there was a message in manly scrawl:

No one gets out of the woods faster than you.

Hope that's true for your tummy ache too.
Let me make it up to you?
~ G

Just who are you, George Springs? she wondered.

That was two years ago. The porcupine-moose-wolf incident – which never appeared in the *Trib* – replayed in George's mind that West Virginia morning as he held the can of pepper spray. Like Montana, he didn't need to use it. Like Montana, he climbed the summit alone and pocketed his rock. Like Montana, the instant he returned to his office, he placed it in a display cabinet that hung on his wall. He labeled it "Spruce Knob, West Virginia: Elevation 4,863 feet – 09-15-12." He admired it (with the other rocks on display) at length over morning coffee, lost in a feeling that money couldn't buy – a feeling that often eluded him. And just like his return from Montana – 16 states ago – when he finally sat down behind his desk, there, taped to his telephone, impossible to miss, was a hand-written note from Paige. This one was a response to his invitation to accompany him to a charity event the following week:

Have I ever said no? One little black dress coming right up.

Chapter 5

Is there anything more telling than a cause? A food drive, an adopted stretch of highway, a soul to save – any of a hundred acts that require more resolve than deliberation. A cause ultimately invokes the very thing it reveals: a human heart. In his 33 years, George had volunteered exactly once, and then only because the mayor had pressed. No one said no to the mayor. Not in a mafia town. Shoulder to shoulder, they spooned mashed potatoes at the homeless shelter the previous Thanksgiving. George's *only* cause was Love by George.

But after matchmaking for a decade, his passion for his craft had begun to wane. Shooting commercial after commercial had taken its toll – all that smiling in the spotlight, hours of it at a time, delivering scripted words in full makeup. Off camera, he put in 80 to 100 hours a week, sometimes more. To recharge, he sought areas without cell phone reception, drawn to the quiet. But even off-radar, he was badgered, most frequently in public restrooms. Nothing challenged his patience more than making small talk with strangers while urinating. Nothing except the stack of "Unmatchables."

Every dating service suffered them. Unmatchables sailed through compatibility tests, scored potential matches, then tragically spoke. They used topics like biological clocks as icebreakers. Or proposed within five minutes of a first hello. First dates were always the last, a quandary for any dating service selling itself on successfully matching clients. At least once a month, the Unmatchable profiles on George's desk left his brain with stretch marks.

"What about a dating class for the Unmatchables?" George

asked Ted one day over lunch. "We gotta' do something: Teach these guys not to over-cologne, body hair removal, what not to wear. And teach the ladies to hush up about wedding plans and baby talk."

"Good luck with that," said Ted, dipping an egg roll in sweet and sour sauce. But it was an idea he couldn't dismiss. A higher percentage of client matches was the only relevant industry statistic. It would mean graduating from the found-my-soul-mate commercials to advertising hard numbers. It meant propelling Love by George past its competitors. It meant a possible raise for Ted if it worked.

"Just something I've been toying with," said George. "Here. Take a peek." He handed Ted a cocktail napkin with the scribbled words: *There was nothing she didn't want. So, I took her to the bakery for an Everything Bagel. When she complained after the first bite, I knew she was trouble.'* "It's an icebreaker, a way to get the conversation started," explained George. "After that, we hit them with dating do's and don'ts. Workbook exercises, role play …."

"Role play? For men? That'll be the day. I realize that not sounding like an idiot is a learned skill for this lot, but role play? Maybe for ladies."

"Forget gender. Male or female, they can't be matched for a reason. They need help looking and sounding normal. They need practice."

"They need therapy, but we can't prescribe that. Look, if you are serious, you had better plant a couple of hotties. These guys would give *anything* to sit next to a hottie and try to form words. Better yet, make the instructor a hottie. And just to be clear, by hottie, I mean a woman. A man cannot teach a class like this. The moment he says anything about hygiene or fashion, the ladies will verbally assault him. And God help him if he mentions socks."

"Socks?"

Ted shook his head. "Forget it."

"So you think we need a woman's touch?"

"Touch, feel and looks." Ted tossed George a fortune cookie. "On second thought, better make her a semi-hottie. If she's too hot, the ladies in class will just want to rip out her hair. A semi-hottie is less risky – more of an inspiration than a threat. We need her charms to trickle down. Someone to teach them how to bulge their eyes and suck in their cheeks. You know, girl stuff."

George chuckled. "You, my friend, are a lawsuit waiting to happen. Good thing we have Hal."

"You will need that attorney's services before I do. Just go with the semi-hottie. I'm right about this. And for God's sake, get one that's not all pierced and tattooed. Hard to find one like that in this day and age, I know, but we have an image to uphold. Come to think of it, I interviewed a clean one like that last week. Feisty little thing. She *might* work. It would probably take some convincing. I hadn't planned on calling her back."

"New plan. Bring the semi-hottie on board."

Later that afternoon, Madeline, George's secretary, left early for a doctor's appointment. Calls poured into George's office unfiltered – solicitations, media requests, troubled clients. George was left holding the phone. He welcomed the distraction at first, but it wasn't long before yawning replaced his enthusiasm. He countered with coffee and occupied his free hand by folding and unfolding his fortune cookie message. *That's odd,* he thought, skimming the words. *Did Confucius run out of quotes?* The messaging was most un-fortune-cookie-like: words penned by Emily Dickinson, a poem about feathers and perches, beginning on one side of the paper, finishing on the flip side. At 5 p.m. he hung up, tossed the fortune into his desk drawer and grabbed his keys. The phone rang again. He picked it up and muttered hello.

The caller requested an entire evening – red carpet, black tie, invitation only for a $1,000-a-plate fundraiser for The First Orphanage of Chicago. "With *you* as the keynote speaker," the caller pleaded, "we could raise next year's operating budget in a single night. You were our first choice. Pretty please."

A master at saying no, George did not say it this time. He didn't even bother checking his itinerary before agreeing.

And so, three weeks later, right after West Virginia, he tuxedo-ed up and slipped through the side door of Loft on Lake in the Downtown West Loop. The event organizer led him backstage, behind a velvety red curtain. Together, they watched a pigtailed redhead stand on her tippy toes and speak into the microphone. "Someday, I hope to have my own bedroom," she said, "and bedtime stories and a mommy and daddy cheering for me at soccer games. Someday. Maybe." An unspoken "but maybe not" was implied in her fragile voice. She looked down at the stage floor, walked to her front row seat and sat. Her words stifled the air. Some in the audience clapped in hesitance, uncertain if applause was appropriate. Others dabbed at tears.

Anxious to move things along, the emcee announced George Springs the Third and motioned him onto stage. When George opened his mouth to speak, his usual shtick – a bottomless bag of slash-and-burn dating tales – did not come out. "Well, I …," he stammered. "No getting past that now, is there?" With the spotlight glaring and cameras flashing, he gripped the podium with both hands, bowed his head and attempted to find the transition between the dreams and disappointments of orphans and his prepared remarks. "Sorry. I guess this just hits a little too close to home." He winked at the little girl, then held up a note card in his hand. "I won't tell you how much time I spent rehearsing these jokes. But clearly, a few laughs aren't going to fix *this*. I occupied one of those seats, once." He pointed to the row of orphans. "I know. Impossible, right? Only it isn't. Twenty-five years ago, that was me. Well, me minus the pigtails."

Jaws dropped. Was this a joke? No one knew squat about George's past – not so-called friends, not acquaintances, no one. Many marveled at his ability to duck the press and keep his personal life private. Now this: Orphan George.

He continued – talking about the family down the street from his childhood foster home. They ate chocolate chip cookies for breakfast, played board games around the fireplace and did not let five minutes pass without laughing. The love in that house made it a home. He wanted to stay there. He felt like he belonged. And then, without warning, that family left, shortly after the For Sale sign appeared in their front yard. For George, what stuck was a picture of how a family ought to be, a family he never had. "That's what these kids deserve," he said in closing. "And we are in a position to help. Whatever you donate tonight, I will double it. So you tell me: What's it going to be?"

A thunderous ovation followed.

At the after party, George attempted to repel the cameras single-handedly since Paige and her little black dress disappeared. Nothing bored her more than *other* reporters. "I need a drink," she whispered before abandoning him, flashing her good side for photographers. Orphan George was news to her too, but nowhere near as intriguing as his net worth.

"Were you an orphan from birth?" one reporter inquired, shoving a microphone in George's face.

"Were you unwanted?" asked another.

"Is that why you aren't married?" yet another pressed. "Do you fear commitment?"

George loathed such intrusions, and Paige lost points for not rescuing him. "Don't suppose I could interest you in dancing," she could have said, or something equally tactful then whisked him away.

"Can't keep the lady waiting," George would have answered, dusting the reporters in vogue.

But there was zero chance of that happening, he knew. Their pairing was a mutual convenience, nothing more. As the face of Love by George, he could not be seen at social gatherings alone without provoking inquiry. "No date for Mr. Compatibility?" people would say. Such talk was bad for business. So, when

George could not avoid the limelight, he called Paige. He had not yet found a suitable replacement after their first date.

To Paige, the principle highlight of *that* date, the first one, now two years ago, was the fact that it was indoors and far removed from wild animals. However, that night too began poorly: with a deficiency of doting over her ecru sheath dress – sleeveless, cut above the knees, attire intended to set George howling. She looked better than any man deserved with her hair pulled back and punchy lips that matched her fire brick sling backs. And she owned every bit of it walking out the door to George's car.

"Nice outfit," he said upon seeing her.

Never before had her appearance elicited such scant praise. *He will learn*, she thought. But as the evening progressed, she concluded otherwise. When together, George turned more heads than she did. The mere sight of him arrested the public: his slate-colored hair all slicked back, muscular jaw and sparkling cobalt eyes. Not to mention his celebrity status. Without uttering a word, he breathed life into a room. In his company, Paige was a footnote. As if that weren't enough, the sound of his baritone voice sapped whatever strength remained in feminine knees – every woman, it seemed, except Paige. Melting was beneath her. So was not being the center of attention. But for a man with pockets as deep as George's, she convinced herself that she could make an exception.

"Oh Georgie," she cooed after he delivered a joke that night at the museum social, "you missed your calling. You should have done stand up."

Without expression, he looked at her and said nothing.

The next hour, they spent weaving in and out of small talk – a mix of donors, museum curators and academia. A lisping geologist warned that the world was running out of rocks. The claim prompted an even duller tangent from a human factors research scientist. Paige placed her palm between George's shoulder blades and gently worked her fingernails. His sideways glance eventually led to a full head turn. She bit her lip and flashed pouty eyes.

George responded with Mona Lisa flair: Maybe it was a smile. Maybe it was gas.

Paige continued the delicate exercise of attempting to turn him. "You sure work a lot, Georgie," she said. "I'm pretty sure that on our death beds, none of us will say, 'Gee, I wish I had worked more.'"

"No. I suppose not," George conceded.

"What *will* we wish for? I wonder."

Again George made no reply.

Later, he didn't attempt a kiss goodnight. He may have forgotten her altogether if not for a state senator's hastily assembled meet-and-greet four weeks later. George, himself, was to host the event at his personal residence – a payback, from the sound of it. "I'd like my favorite *Trib* reporter at my side," said George, "for pleasure, of course, not in an official capacity."

Paige was tempted to say, "I'll check my schedule and get back to you," but thought better of it. With sing-song theatrics, she accepted. But this time, she wouldn't stoop. The burn marks from their first date had not yet healed. Her new ploy was to ignore him completely. After hours of indifference and a few martinis, she would throw him a bone – a look that even the dumbest animal could interpret. Pulling it off required George to take note of her inattention, to be alarmed, then annoyed, then brood, then look once more for the payoff. Brilliant as it was in concept, in action, it fizzled. It proved to be entirely too much exercise for George's neck. If he attempted eye contact more than once that night, she missed it.

By the time date three rolled around, reality had sunk in. If George had thoughts of getting married and misbehaving like other millionaires, he kept them to himself. He needed an escort, nothing more. Instead of wasting herself on him, Paige used their outings to sniff out the second most eligible bank roll.

That's why Orphan George fielded the questions alone at the fundraiser, a dozen dates after their first. "No comment," he said repeatedly. "This isn't about me tonight." Reporters did not relent until he pointed to a tray of circulating hors d'oeuvres and said, "I can't believe that you are wasting time on me when there's foie gras." When they turned in search of the once-banned delicacy, George made his escape.

Finding Paige was not difficult. He just followed the giggling. She had stepped outside with a coterie of admirers. It didn't take someone in the dating business to translate her intent. "... Aren't you the sweetest thing, Wilfred," she said to a man old enough to be her father. "If you're lying, don't stop. My, how these fundraisers make a girl thirsty. With all this gentle *man*-hood around, you'd think someone would notice an empty glass. Now which one of you ...."

Suddenly, her eyes detected George. Her body reacted as it always did when jolted: with hiccups. She stood and gawked and lurched every four seconds. George's appearance dispersed the tuxedos like foiled magpies. Only he and Paige remained.

Again Mona Lisa smiled. Then he drove Paige home.

Chapter 6

By age 30, Hope had drawn the conclusion that in life, give and take is mostly give. And as time progressed, it meant giving up things that made the journey worthwhile. Things like whole milk in her coffee. Like a cigarette afterward. Like believing that any man could be trusted with her heart.

She had soared through her 20s needing nothing more than a foo foo cup of joe and a smoke to cope with anything. But after her 30th birthday, genetics changed that. Bad LDLs and HDLs riddled her mother's side of the family. Flagged for high cholesterol, Hope scheduled an appointment with her family practitioner one day between dropping of resumes.

"Let's not try medication yet," said Dr. Hoshimoto. "You're young. I suggest altering your diet. If you can't give up your macchiatos, then try oatmeal for breakfast. Let's see what that does to your numbers." The oatmeal he prescribed was whole-grain, un-sugared, made with skim milk, to be ingested by the gloppy spoonful.

"Um, texture problem," objected Hope. "I only do oatmeal in cookie form. What's the monster cookie equivalent of a bowl of oatmeal?"

Hoshimoto frowned. "Zero. If oatmeal is out, you need to eliminate the Half-and-Half. Switch to soy milk or drink water instead of coffee. And reduce your intake of fried foods and fatty snacks." Next, he pulled out a chart showing that every cigarette smoked subtracted 11 minutes from her life.

No more cigarettes? thought Hope. *And how many minutes a day do I lose from having nothing to look forward to?* Thankfully, the good doctor did not diagnose the inner workings of her heart. It was predisposed to be given completely or not given at all. For that, there was no remedy.

Nor had Hope found an agreeable substitute for texting while driving. Chicago had recently banned it. *Ridiculous!* thought Hope. Windy City logic escaped her. In the 1970s, Chicago had banned pinball machines. Pinball machines! Now texting was in the crosshairs. What next, oxygen? What's a girl to do in a city of 8 million in glacially slow traffic? One can only listen to music so long. She hadn't the nerves for talk radio. Urban scenery may have inspired Carl Sandburg's poetry, but not hers. There was *no* substitute for texting. Three weeks after her interview with Ted, in bumper-to-bumper traffic, she broke the law and texted April: *people, warts & all, sometimes surprise.*

"What people?" asked April, telephoning her back as Hope pulled into her condo.

"Mom inspired that. I stopped by to see her after picking up some more job applications. I was being all neurotic about finding work. She was actually pretty great about listening and not rolling her eyes – a first, I think. Anyway, it stopped me from calling you for reassurance that my life still has purpose. What's news there?"

"No rats in the Gucci bag today. Nothing more to report, really. Except, well, later today, I might have something."

"What's with the might? That's not how this works. I frighten you with full disclosure. You reciprocate. Then we lie to each other about how it's all going to be okay. It's called friendship. Oh, there's a beep. Hang on. Got another call."

"I have to go anyway."

"You're not off the hook with the might. Bye." She pushed a button and took the next call.

"Hope?" a familiar voice said. "Hi. It's Mary."

"Um."

"Mary Stevens from Love by George. We met a few weeks ago when you interviewed. I'm Mr. Marble's secretary. You remember Ted?"

"Of course," said Hope. *Like I could ever forget him.*

"Good news! I am pleased to offer you the marketing position that you applied for." She relayed how impressive Ted had said she was during the interview, then finished with "congratulations" and "seventy thousand a ye-owch!"

"Everything okay?"

"One moment please." Under routine duress, Mary could melodically suppress any discomfort. Not today. Not after Ted bumped her chair while eavesdropping. The jolt forced her inner thighs to touch, rekindling the scourge of New Orleans.

It was Mary's first day back from an administrative conference in the Big Easy. Her trip there began with severe turbulence. Bonus frequent flyer miles were doled out for passengers who whined the loudest. Mary was not among them. There simply wasn't time. She had every minute planned before the conference began at noon: Bourbon Street, Jackson Square, the St. Louis Cathedral, beignets at Café du Monde. Everything was within walking distance of the hotel. What better way to spend a September morning?

But New Orleans is not Chicago, not the right climate to stop powdering after the armpits, especially in 90-degree weather. And the travel brochures had not warned against wearing denim. Canal Street was a sauna. The air clung to Mary's petite frame, activating long-dormant sweat glands. Two blocks after exiting the hotel, every inch of her dripped. Determined, she soldiered on, crinkling her nose at the stench of stale tobacco, liquor and century-old building decay.

In Jackson Square, a rash broke out between her legs. It compromised her gait, turning her bow-legged. She immediately scratched the remainder of her itinerary. Her thighs chafed at the panty line. When she made it back to her hotel room, she realized that she had forgotten to pack baby powder. Unable to purchase any before the conference began, she burned all day long.

"Not much time for sight-seeing," she told co-workers dismissively, that same morning she phoned Hope. It was true enough. The only way that she could have taken in more of the French Quarter would have been in a skirt, riding in a wheelchair, with her legs cracked. She would rather have died. Instead, she holed up in her hotel room each night and worked her way down the room-service salad menu in search of something with flavor. What she really needed after New Orleans was a vacation, not an in-your-face Ted tasking her with hiring Hope for "as cheap as possible."

"Start at seventy thousand a year," he had instructed. "And make it sound generous." Mary kept her smile until Ted bumped her chair.

Through the receiver, Hope heard Ted say "oops!" and Mary whisper something about purchasing a voodoo doll in his likeness. Next, Ted snarled, "... getting harder and harder to find good, cheap help."

"Excuse me," said Mary, finally addressing Hope again. "That's seventy thousand a year. What do you say?"

"Something tells me that seventy thousand doesn't quite compensate for the personal suffering there. Tell you what, I'll kick it around and get back to you." Flattered, she hung up and phoned April with the news and then her parents. Despite the previous day's breakthrough – when maternal empathy materialized from thin air – her mother processed this new information like raw meat. "You turned down how much?" she barked. "Your mortgage isn't going to pay itself!" An assisted living accountant, her mother righteously stewed over lost revenue, that is, unless some poor codger died on schedule. "It's okay," she would assure her boss on such occasions. "I budgeted for his death." In other words, after reviewing clients' ages and health conditions, she had accurately predicted the time of their passing, which meant that the company was still on budget. She did not, however, budget for her daughter rejecting $70,000 a year.

"Remind me again why I tell you anything, Mom."

Eventually, Hope's father, a retired drill sergeant, wrestled away the phone. "Ignore your mother, honey," he said. "She can't help it. Just follow your gut. We both want you to be happy."

"Give me that, cream puff!" snapped Hope's mother, yanking away the phone. "And to think that you used to train soldiers for combat."

At precisely that moment, Half-a-Donut Mary called again. This time, Love by George offered $80,000.

"Dunno," replied Hope, her tone bordering on flippancy. "I still need time to think."

Half an hour later, a third call. "Ninety thousand," said Mary. "Final offer."

"Ninety, huh?" repeated Hope. She wanted to tell Ted to shove it, but something inside wouldn't allow it. "Final offer," she knew, meant now or never. "Can't say no to that now, can I? Unless, of course, Ted plans on being my supervisor. That would be a deal-breaker for me."

"Please hold." Hope strained to hear the ensuing discussion, which, but for the unmistakable splintering of Ted's voice, was indecipherable. A full two minutes later, Mary spoke into the receiver again, saying the last thing that Hope expected. "We agree to those terms. You will report directly to the owner, George Springs. You start Tuesday morning at 8 o'clock sharp."

"Ohhh-kayyyyyy. Uh, Tuesday, not Monday? At eight?"

"Well, around here, it's not a bad idea to show up five minutes early. And yes, Tuesday. See you then." Mary's voice lowered to an undertone. "Good call on the supervisor." Click.

Seriously? thought Hope. *They just hired me?* Never before had she been so irreverent with an employer. There was no understanding it, and April wasn't answering her phone to help make sense of things. *Where could she be?*

Halfway across town, April was soliciting.

"You've got two minutes, lady," said a shop owner – bespectacled, balding, bloodshot eyes from staring at a computer too long. "So what's this? And why should I give it shelf space?"

April nudged a bronze, plate-sized gong forward on the counter. "*This* is a must have," she said, referencing a recipe card. "I'm new at this. I need to stick to my script. This is a guaranteed meeting shortener. And who among us doesn't need shorter meetings? Place this gong somewhere in a meeting room and when the inevitable happens – when someone opens his mouth and out comes stupid – wham!" She waved an ordinary looking ballpoint pen like a drum stick. The gong, which had STUPID engraved across it in all caps, crashed and vibrated. "Here. You try." She offered the clerk a pen. He grabbed it, snapped his wrist and flashed a toothy grin when the gong crashed again. "A thing of beauty, no?" said April. "If this doesn't end the meeting drivel, nothing will. Four pens per gong. Extra four packs of pens available. Batteries included."

Nearby shoppers buzzed with approval.

"Clever," said the shop owner, opening his till. "I'll take ten STUPID gongs. And leave a card. I might want more."

April flipped through a stack of $20 bills on her way out and crossed the Michigan Avenue curio shop off her list. Her next solicitation was another quick sale. And the next. By mid-afternoon, her sixth stop of the day, her inventory was depleted. She wanted to tell Hope, but not yet.

Friends don't leave friends n the dark, apes.

Hope's last text read, one of four attempts that afternoon to extract information. Hope continued to put the squeeze on until sunset, when she stopped by April's apartment and walked in on a surprise congrats-on-the-new-job soiree: party favors, appetizers, wine and four of Hope's dearest friends.

"So this is what you've been up to," said Hope. The gathering was precisely what she needed: some wine tasting, giggling and unladylike tangents. It distracted her from Tuesday morning, until she opened the office-warming gifts – a desk clock, a spider plant and a frilly gift bag from April.

"Still trying to convert me, I see," said Hope, digging through tissue paper, finding a candle. She hoisted it like a trophy. Several months before, she had scolded April for blowing $500 at a candle party.

April defended her purchase – praising the virtues of soy, flamelessness and breakthrough slow-burning technology. "This one is my favorite," she had said, holding a white and red pillar candle.

Hope took a whiff. "You *like* that smell?"

"It's called *Blood Kiss*. It's a vampire thing."

Hope let it go. *What good can come from combining wax and perfume and contrived names?* she wondered. After the *Blood Kiss* experience, she found herself picking up candles – usually at greeting card stores – sniffing, christening them aloud, then checking their given names. Time and again, what she called *Grandma Emptied the Perfume Bottle* was named *Heirloom Pearls* or something equally lame.

Tonight, the candle that April presented her with was nectarine in color. Hope held it to her nose. "Citrus Tequila," she guessed before flipping it over and reading the sticker. "Love Spell? Oh I get it: Love Spell ... Love by George. It's an industry candle. I'm set now. I shall diligently fan its flamelessness until online love redeems the terminally single."

The conversation then turned to attire. After some deliberation, party guests reached consensus regarding what Hope should wear her first day on the job. "Don't forget: button-down white collar shirt with the black pant suit," April reminded her when they said goodbye.

"Thanks for this," said Hope, squeezing her on the way out. "I'm all better now."

But doubt returned during the drive home, as it always did in solitude. *Why in the world are they paying me $90,000 a year? It makes no sense. Guess all I can do is put on the black pant suit tomorrow morning and walk through that door.*

Chapter 7

Shakespeare moments. We all have them, everyday illuminations between tragedy and poetry and wit. Hope's first enlightenment the next morning occurred before 7:00 a.m. "*To coffee, perchance to awaken,*" she posted on Facebook after donning her black pant suit. In jitters, she left her condo for day one at Love by George, wondering how anyone could adopt a decaffeinated lifestyle. *A greeting card just died,* she thought when she backed out of her driveway, imagining the hours to come, the hours of not writing poetry, of not selling greeting cards. *Ninety thousand a year. For what?* She turned on the radio, adjusted the knob and found a saxophone with a medicinal effect.

Twenty minutes later, she shuffled into the coffee shop. "Tall Gazebo, no room," said the man standing at the cash register. He wore a three-piece suit and spoke with a dark timbre.

"Sorry," said the cashier, distracted with changing the receipt tape. "Didn't catch that."

"Tall Gazebo, no room." He folded up a newspaper, tucked it under his arm and reached for his wallet.

The cashier nodded. "Tall Gazebo, no room," she repeated, muffling a yawn.

"Tall Gazebo, no room," chanted the barista, confirming the order. Her eyes were vacant saucers, unseeing, yet fixed on the espresso machine in front of her.

With a smirk, Hope turned toward the back of the line. "Tall Gazebo, no room," she echoed in her best Gregorian monk, matching the employees' enthusiasm level.

"Don't make me hop the counter, No Fun," warned the

cashier, wagging her finger. "I do the mocking around here. The usual for you today?"

"You know me so ...," said Hope. *Hello!* She spun around again in time to witness a batty-eyed blonde climbing all over Green Eyes, who had just stepped into line. "... well," continued Hope, deflated. "It's too early in the morning for this."

"Downright pukish if you ask me," the barista agreed. "No way to start the day."

In solidarity they glared, despising. The bimbo looked Scandinavian – an all-natural bouncy honey-butter blonde with horse-like teeth, one of those vile creatures who clearly didn't need caffeine. She played with Green Eyes' scarf like he was a dress-up toy and cooed in single syllables. The stimulation brightened his cheeks to a rosy glow. He couldn't take his eyes off her even if the coffee shop were on fire.

"How about topping my drink off with whip cream today?" muttered Hope.

"You got it! Want me to throw gum in her hair too while I'm at it?"

"Oh, would you? And they say customer service is dead."

The barista handed Hope her drink. "Not here. Off to work now?"

"Yes, sadly."

"And where is work?"

Hope shook her head. "You wouldn't believe me if I told you. I'm not sure I believe it myself."

Coffee in hand, Hope entered the John Hancock Center for $90,000-a-year day one. Mac met her again at the elevator. "I had a feeling I would be seeing more of ye," he said, his eyes glinting. "How 'bout a quick dash tuh the top later? Over lunch, per'aps? Clear skies t'day. Ye can see the whole downtown spread."

"I'll have to take a rain check," answered Hope. "Floor 37 is my threshold today." *What is it with this guy and the top floor?* She needed to focus on other things now, like her chest. During her last ascent in that elevator, it was coffee-stained and smoking. Not today. She checked and double checked.

Today, Madeline, George's secretary, not Karli, received her at the front desk. The office tour began after Hope filled out her W-4. "I understand you've already met Ted," she said, sidestepping the corner office, not expecting a reply, not getting one. "I hope that you reserve your judgment about the rest of us until you are better acquainted." The introductions that followed – with customer service, accounting and the marketing departments – were all fluid and obliging, but left Hope feeling the burden of expectation. So did her new digs.

No way! she thought, upon entering her office. *My own wall of windows!* When Madeline left her, Hope settled behind the desk and swiveled her chair, taking in the foot traffic below, a scene that could easily have inspired a literary vignette. She powered on her computer. Waiting for it to boot, she returned to the doorway and peeked out. *Empty hallway.* She slid her fingers across the letters on the name plate – Hope Allday, Director of Marketing. *I guess this isn't a joke after all. I work for an online dating service now, for reasons known only to Ted, George and God himself.*

Five minutes later, Madeline reappeared. "George had planned on welcoming you today," she said, placing a file on her desk. "Something came up. Something always does. Anyway, he wanted me to give you this. It'll make sense if you read his email first. I'm just down the hall if you need anything. Welcome aboard. I hope you like it here. We've *all* heard such great things about you."

All? thought Hope with a gulp, recalling the dirt that Ted had dug up. *Did you circulate a bubble bath and Barry Manilow memo?*

George's e-mail read: So pleased that you accepted our offer. LBG is lucky to have you. You'll be hitting the ground running. Priority one: the Unmatchables, clients that have trouble getting second and third dates. You'll be teaching a class for them on

Fridays – starting this Friday – but don't sweat it. The only Week 1 expectation is survival. This class is your baby. Long-term goal: help them get more dates. No timeline. Just keep me posted: attendance figures, game plan, results, etc. I've included a few ideas to get you started. Madeline is at your disposal. ~ G

"This Friday?" said Hope aloud. *I'm the instructor? What do I know about matching people? I can't even match myself.* The file contained a company history, two years of annual reports and a green folder labeled "The Unmatchables."

Needing a moment to process, she zombied down the corridor for another shot of caffeine, not expecting to find Ted in the break room. He stood in front of the coffee machine, his head twisting backward, eyeballing his posterior from multiple angles.

"Everything okay?" asked Hope timidly.

"Fine," he snapped. He dropped a creamer container, accidentally on purpose. "Got it!" he shouted, stretching out his elbows as though securing the area. After snatching it off the floor, he retreated down the hallway, mumbling. His day had begun with Mary saying, "nice pants." Taking her words literally was impossible after the Sock Nazi incident. *It's the pants now, is it?* he thought. "Nice pants" was a comment he, himself, would make after seeing another man wearing red pants or capris. "Nice pants" meant "Is the circus in town?" Today he was wearing black slacks, not something deserving of insinuation. Stomping off after Mary's remark, he conducted a self-exam in the break room: checking his zipper first, then scanning for stains and clinging fabric softeners. The exact moment that he made eye contact with his rear end – assuming solitude – Hope appeared.

"Checking yourself out there, huh Ted?" Hope could have asked. *Why didn't I say that?* she thought, now filling her coffee cup. *Guess I'll just have to console myself with the fact that he's probably losing sleep over not being my supervisor and paying me $20,000 a year more than he wanted.*

Back at her desk, Hope began crafting a response to George's email. *'Sorry I didn't get a chance to meet you in person,'* she began. Staring at the cursor, she thought *now what?*

Her cell phone vibrated: a text from her father. *We lost our Barbie Doll today,* it read. The "lost" texts were a decade-plus-old tradition. They began in the late 1990s with *"We lost our Princess today."*

lost? i'm still here. Hope had replied back then, before learning of Lady Di's death. When she died, her father texted, and the "lost" celebrity death game began.

Today, it was Barbara. *Bush, Mandrell, Eden, Boxer?* wondered Hope. *Oh, I know!* She typed *walters?* Barbara Walters looked remarkable for a woman her age, Hope thought. Not quite Raquel Welch remarkable, but somewhere in the same universe. No Botox blunders. A timeless elegance about her, probably from the ability to spin bad news into something worth watching. Hope hit send then checked her next message.

2 hours and nary a peep, April texted. *running the company yet? love by hope. poetic. could be big.*

Hope replied: *more like unmatchables by hope. poetry not included. wait til u hear this 1.* Her cell phone vibrated again, signaling her father's reply.

Not Walters. Billingsley, it read. *Beaver's mom. Remember? You used to sit on my lap after school & watch re-runs.*

forget? typed Hope. *nev-uh! will always b your little girl. smooches & squeezes.* She cracked open the Unmatchables file once more and rifled through the 20-page report. It included a profile of the average Unmatchable, tables, graphs and various other attachments. Lesson plan one (the only lesson plan included) outlined an hour's worth of activities: introductions, George's Everything Bagel Exercise and a personal pledge sheet. Bizarre as it was to read, it made sense. Tear down the Unmatchables. Rid them of turn offs. Turn them loose and measure the results. *Maybe I CAN do this,* thought Hope. Riding the maybe, she finished typing her response to George:

Just finished the Unmatchables file. My first report will be on your desk by noonish on Monday. Your 2 cents from time to time will be helpful, so I know I'm on the right track. ~ H

If he is "G," she thought, *I'm "H."*

The balance of the day, and the next two, Hope sifted through the 25 registered class members' profiles. They *seemed* normal on paper: normal pastimes, normal wish lists, normal family values. *My seemer must off,* she thought. *What am I missing here?* It was a question that could only be answered in person.

On Friday, the first Unmatchable to arrive was Bill, sporting a flowery, double-pocketed western shirt, corduroy bell bottoms and flip flops. With a long, thinning blond tangle of hair, he strutted across the room like a potbellied peacock. He clicked his tongue and pointed at Hope then eased into a chair. Margaret came next in mascara-gone-wild eyes and a tube top-sweat suit ensemble: blue top, yellow cotton pants with elastic ankles and tube socks that disappeared into snow-white Crocs.

Do these people not own mirrors? wondered Hope, aghast. After watching the room fill, she grew to doubt it. So disturbed was she at the show of fabric – her own periwinkle skirt suit notwithstanding – that it took her quite some time to maintain eye contact.

Then they spoke – more guys than girls at first. "I have a love-love relationship with your bangs," said one Unmatchable, puckering up.

This was in reply to Hope's introductory statement: "I have a love-hate relationship with my bangs." Her remark was intended to demonstrate that she too was human, that she too had frustrations, that she too was less than perfect. "Let's just clear something up right now," replied Hope. "I am *not* dating anyone in this class. So, no hitting on me. Got it? Other questions?"

"More of a validation, really," said Bill. "What do you think of this?" He held up a laminated card that read:

1 – The Unmentionable
2 – Greetings: hi-ya, ciao, etc.
3 – Compliments: you're amazing, lovely, look nice, etc.
4 – Feelings: I miss you, ache for you, etc.

"What's this?" asked Hope.

"I thought that was obvious," replied Bill. "It's texting code. My own creation. I only get 158 characters per text, not a lot of real estate. So I condensed frequently-used communications into numbers. I am an actuary by trade, a numbers guy. I prefer numbers to words. Numbers are more concise than words. And I find them less boring in repetition. You like?"

"Am I to understand, that rather than telling a woman – possibly your future wife –that you ache for her or miss her, you text her the number four instead?"

"Ding, ding, ding! I knew you could figure it out. See? Obvious." Turning to the rest of the class, he held up another card and added, "Plenty more where that came from, guys. Wallet-sized. Yours for a buck."

"You're killing me, Bill. Something tells me you've never actually loved."

"Love? What's so special about love? *Anyone* can love. I recently read that scientists chemically identified brain-reaction compounds for every emotion, including love, or the Unmentionable – number one on my chart. But love is just one compound in the brain, one of the inferior compounds if you ask me, not nearly as interesting as aching, a class four feeling. I almost gave it its own number. Ever ache for someone, teach?"

"Uh." Hope traversed the floor and looked out the window before facing Bill again. "Of course. Hasn't everyone? But what about the rest of you? What other questions do you have?"

"Just one," said Margaret, in the blue tube top. "How do I cope after losing the only one who made me happy? I mean I know it was only one date three months ago, but it was real."

"No one can *make* you happy," said Hope. The rebuke

surprised her. It came off her lips convincingly, like a reflex, as it did when her college psyche professor said it during a lecture years ago. Only now it sounded smart. "Wrong question," she continued. "The real question is why do you *choose* to let others dictate your happiness?"

"I can't believe you are teaching this class," interjected Betty, crossing her arms. "Obviously, *you* have never truly loved."

Hope stared back, paralyzed.

"Oh don't look at me like that," continued Betty. "Just because I'm sitting in a chair and you're standing up there doesn't mean that I have never loved. I have. Hearts either race or thud. There is no in between. No substitute for someone who improves you without uttering a word. If we could simply *choose* that kind of happiness, we wouldn't be here today."

Hope braced herself on the nearest desk and checked the wall clock. *Fifty minutes left?* Her knees felt like she was on the elevator again. She retreated to the podium and flipped through her lesson planner. "Lively discussion, but I think we're getting ahead of ourselves. We haven't even been properly introduced. I need to hear more about *you*. What landed *you* here today? What are *your* goals? *Your* expectations? Let's start with *you*, Betty."

Skipping the Everything Bagel Exercise, Hope thought as Betty introduced herself. *It might lead to more leeching of my credibility.* The introductions wrapped up just as the hour ended. Hope had milked them for all they were worth, asking any question to keep students talking, to keep the focus on them, not her. After class, her body screamed for something stronger than aspirin.

That evening, over margaritas, she told April about Betty's remark and said, "This isn't going to work. And then there's Bill, the number cruncher. I can't even remember the last time I ached for someone. And he's got a number for it."

In empathy, April polished off the bowl of nachos and salsa and flagged down the waiter for seconds. Twice, she interjected,

"You did your best. What more can you do?" Hope refuted her, listing every reason that she was unqualified to instruct. "Sounds impossible," replied April. "I wouldn't even know where to begin."

"Grooming was all I could think of when I saw them."

"Gotta' start somewhere."

Hope dipped a chip and shrugged. *Why not?* she thought. *George gave me the green light to do whatever I want.*

Hope's mind spun. She arose the next day still meditating on fashion. The contemplation worked itself into an Unmatchables Report that required no thought – ideas going forward, not the lowlights of Friday's class. After completing it Monday morning, she deposited it in George's inbox on his desk. A wave of triumph swelled within her. *Near perfection,* she thought. *And ahead of schedule.* With the lights off and no one around, she picked up the white candle next to his computer. "And what's your scent, Mr. Compatibility?" she said aloud, holding it to her nose. Shutting her eyes, she inhaled. "Hotel bed sheets!"

A gasp from behind startled her. Madeline stood in the doorway, a hand covering her mouth. Behind her, Ted and George craned their necks.

Hotel bed sheets? repeated Hope's inner voice, sounding like it had just swallowed helium. *Did you really just say that out loud? Quick, say something else. Save yourself.* "Clean ones!" her voice crackled.

More craning. Another gasp.

Hope's eyes swelled. *Just kill me!* Crimson-cheeked, she fled, parting the trio in a fantastic clicking of heels down the hallway to her office. Closing her door, she stood with her back against it, clutching the knob with one hand. *Dear God no!* she thought, glancing down. George's candle was in her other hand.

Chapter 8

Why am I still holding this? thought Hope, suddenly recalling the day's horoscope rating – a seven.

Her last seven, the day of her interview, her mother had called back that afternoon to read the horoscope, calling it a teachable moment: "Sevens are iffy," she had said in preface. "Winds of change are blowing in your direction, Pisces, but think twice before adjusting your sails. Stay the course and destiny will find you. See? You should not wear your hair up on a day when sails should not be adjusted."

Ignoring her mother's advice that day was one thing. Declining a $70,000-a-year job offer quite another. "Did you *not* read your horoscope again, today?" her mother had yelled. Newspaper pages ruffled. "Here it is! Opportunity is within your grasp. Reach out and grab it. You won't be disappointed. No do-overs today! And *this* is the day you turn down a steady paycheck? On a no do-overs day? I swear you were switched at birth at the hospital."

"Boy do you have this mom thing down," said Hope. "How about reading the 'How to' tip of the day like I do, instead of the horoscope? You might actually learn something useful there, you know, like how to play nice in the sandbox."

"How to's! That's what you've been wasting your time on? *You* need do's and don'ts, not how to's."

Like DON'T christen the boss' candle, thought Hope now. *I certainly could have used a DON'T like that today.* She retreated to her desk, shoved the candle into a drawer and surfed the internet for Unmatchables' fashion tips.

There was a knock on her door.

Julie from customer service poked her head in. "George is here," she bubbled.

A minute later, a second knock – Sam, this time, from the IT department. "Thirsty?" he asked. "There has been a George sighting! Better bring your jacket. It's cold." He left the door ajar.

Hope got up and shut it. As the latch clicked, there was yet another knock. She twisted the knob, yanked open the door and huffed, "Yes, yes. George is here. Believe me, I kn …. oh!"

Madeline stood outside the doorway, staring back, still wearing a look of incredulity.

"Sorry," said Hope. "I was just working on something. I didn't know it was you."

Madeline pursed her lips. "You have been randomly selected for the all-employee drug and alcohol test. Get your driver's license and come with me."

"Now?" asked Hope, reaching for her billfold. *Is this how they pink slip employees around here?*

Madeline held out a vial. "It won't take long. Just a quickie urine sample."

"Oh. That might be a problem. I just went before, uh … when I, um, dropped off my report."

"That is unfortunate," Madeline replied, continuing down the hallway. "I'll get you something to drink."

Hope stopped and pointed back. "I'll just grab my coffee."

"I can't let you do that. You have to be contained. I'll get your coffee in a minute."

"Contained?"

"I don't know why we say that," chuckled Madeline, her voice softening. "Human resources jargon. I never really thought about how it sounds. Rather barbaric I imagine. Funny. Our attorney, Hal, is responsible for the verbiage. You'll meet him before long. Here we are: the holding room." She opened a door at the end of the hallway. There, inside, thumbing through papers, sat George.

"There she is," he said, standing and extending a hand.

"George Springs."

"Nice to finally meet you," replied Hope, weakly. She shook his hand and dropped her eyes. "Hope Allday."

"Yes. Have a seat. We'll talk in a minute."

Hope slunk down in a chair and monitored the urinalysis technician. His back toward her, he wrote something on a clipboard, then clasped a pen inside his lab coat pocket. *Just fire me now,* thought Hope. *No need to doctor my urine results. Well? Say it already. Hotel bed sheets. That's why we're here.*

Several minutes passed before Madeline returned with coffee. Hope slammed it down, praying it would run right through her. *Why can't my superpower be peeing on command? What's in those papers, George? Time to end this charade.* Shielding her eyes with a hand, she turned and spoke. "I'd screen me for drugs too after that."

"Sorry?" said George, looking up.

"The spectacle I made. In your office. I'd say let's forget it ever happened, but we'd both need our memories wiped for that."

George smirked. "That candle has been sitting on my desk for a year completely neglected, untouched until today. Keep it."

"Oh no! I can't keep your…. Uh, I mean I really don't need a, uh, white one." She interlocked her fingers and squeezed.

"No. I insist. You clearly get more out of it than I do. Sometimes it's the little things. We all could use more little things, I think. You aren't here now because of the candle."

"I'm not?" replied Hope. She chanced an unobstructed look at him, her first.

He had buried his nose in the stack of papers again. His hair was parted perfectly to the left, dandruff-free. "Just a random drug test. Same reason I'm here."

"You mean owning the company doesn't score you an exemption?"

"It's a principle thing," said George, his head surfacing again. "I can't require employees to do this if I don't do it myself. No big deal. I can multi-task in here. I just finished your weekly report. Not exactly what I expected." He paused. "It's *better.* I was thinking the Unmatchables needed a little pep talk, some hand holding, maybe a little push, but I like the direction you're taking. It addresses the real issues, I think, tactfully, of course."

Hope's cheeks flushed. "Tact is an aspiration of mine. Being real comes naturally." She broke his stare, thinking, *Holy! If I look into those baby blues any longer, I'll start slurring words.*

"Your understudies aren't exactly fast learners. Believe me, I know. There are no deadlines with this group. Keep following your instincts. They're good."

Eyes like that deserve an encore, thought Hope. *What color is that? Cobalt? I think I'll call it Holy Crap Blue.* "Will do, Mr. Springs," she said, stealing another glance.

"It's George." Standing up, he waved over the technician. "I have a feeling about you, Hope Allday. Such a name. No wonder you are a poet. Speaking of feelings, I think I have to go now. A pleasure to meet you." With a nod, he exited the room.

I think I just sprouted a feeling myself, thought Hope. Several minutes later, her coffee ran its course, and she successfully filled a vial. An email from George awaited her when she returned to her office.

All: I got pulled for today's random drug test, it read. *See? I do it too. Will have to take a rain check on treating you to coffee. Next time, I'll toss in a pastry. And if I don't see you before the 24th, Happy Turkey Day!*

So that's what Julie and Sam were talking about, thought Hope. *A coffee run.*

he has a feeling about me, she texted April. It had been years since she had a boss. George's holding room words came unexpectedly, a sharp contrast from those of almost every other man in her life – red-pen English professors, volleyball coaches, boyfriends past. None of them, it seemed, had ever been happy with her best. They always wanted something more. Or something different. Or something she was not. George's "feeling" buoyed her: *He likes my ideas,* she mused after texting. *And erases deadlines. And what was that he said again? Better than expected. I liked that part. And he treats employees to coffee and pastries!* She threw herself into lesson planning with a renewed, yet singular focus: teaching the Unmatchables to look in the mirror with a critical eye.

"We're going to mix things up a bit today," she announced as the next class began, "do a little data dive." She pointed to a stack of fashion magazines. "I want you all to grab one of those. Doesn't matter which one. Cut out a picture of a model you would like to date. For the purposes of this exercise, let's assume that he or she is your soul mate. Paste your cut-out onto one of these," she continued, holding up a piece of construction paper. "Next to the picture, I want you to write down two things that you like about what he or she is wearing. Then write down two articles of clothing that you are wearing right now that you would change before meeting him or her in person. Any article of clothing at all, except underwear. And if you're not wearing any, I don't want to know. You have 20 minutes. Go!"

When time expired, discussion began. One Unmatchable held up her poster and said, "I like the way he holds himself."

"Posture *is* a plus," said Hope. "The right clothes will bring out *your* posture."

A male student shared a picture of a catwalk model and said, "That dress makes me want to twirl her."

"What specifically about the dress is appealing?" asked Hope. The class responded beautifully: It gave the body proportion. The cut accented specific features. Fabric and material consistency. Proper fit and accessories. She wrote down responses on the white board, numbering each observation under the heading "Fashion Do's."

Only Bill questioned the exercise. "You've got it all backward, teach. You should show up on the first date looking like a slob. If you land a second date, you're golden. That's the kind of chick you want – one that likes you for you, not for your clothes."

"And how's that working for you so far?" asked Hope.

"Uh."

"You're making my point for me, Bill. We want to call attention to that voluptuous brain of yours, or perhaps a physical feature or two. We don't want little Miss-All-That to notice anything but your best attributes. Part of the reason that you were attracted to your cut-out is because of what she was wearing. So everyone, not just Bill, look at what you're wearing right now. How many of the Fashion Do's are you following?"

Bill raised his hand.

"Yes, Bill. What is it now?"

"Men don't wear outfits. Try threads or ensemble or, I dunno, something not so girly."

"Ensemble?" repeated Hope. "Fine. What if you leave class today and run into your cut-out right outside the building here? Is your look a deal-killer? If so, how will your cut-out, your soul mate, ever get to know what's on the inside? One thing you *can* control is what you wear."

"Solid piece of thinking, teach," conceded Bill, scoping himself out with a fresh eye.

"I'm smarter than I look. Your assignment for next Friday's class: Come dressed in an outfit – or ensemble – that would complement your cut-out. It's as easy as following the Fashion Do's. If you need more tips, I'm passing around an email signup sheet."

Thus began Hope's daily fashion and etiquette pointers:

If the budget allows for only one new outfit, ladies, make it a black pant suit. Make sure it fits perfectly. Tailor it. It's an investment. You are worth it. For the vertically challenged, wide pant legs and a pointy-toed shoe.

OK, fellas: When assembling formalwear – and yes, this means get a suit if you don't have one (not a cheap one, have it altered to fit your body) – never button the bottom jacket button. Never means never. Don't try to understand. Just do it.

18 to 30-somethings: Stop saying LIKE after every word.

You're smarter than you sound. Drop LIKE from your lexicon, and you'll attract a different crowd.

Universal tip: No more cotton, elastic-band ankle sweats. Burn them. Giving them to Goodwill will just make them someone else's problem. The world deserves better. Go with sporty athletic clothes that match and fit properly. Who knows? You might just bump into that special someone at the gym today. Be ready.

The results were immediate: baby steps for some, leaps and bounds for others. By the next Friday – the first of many appropriate-small-talk role play sessions – Hope could look at most of her students without cringing. Wearing white tube socks with dress shoes still needed addressing, but she would get to that.

"No class next week," Hope announced before dismissing that day. "Black Friday is a great excuse to continue updating your wardrobe. And if you go out on a date, don't forget that small talk is no different than fashion: Avoid deal-killers. No talk of medical conditions or weird hobbies. Nothing about marriage or future children. It's a first date. The goal, if you like him or her, is to get a second. Highlight your personality assets. What do your friends like about you? Go there if possible, subtly of course. Keep the conversation aimed at something relatable, like vacations or pets – unless you hoard cats or something. And take interest in your date: Listen. Eye contact. Ask questions, but don't interrogate. And absolutely no bites of your date's dessert unless they offer. Order your own. That's a lot to remember, I know, but I believe in you."

On her way out, Margaret stopped and embraced Hope. "Thank you," she said. "I got a second date. Pretty sure it was the black pant suit."

The confession headlined Hope's weekly Unmatchables Report. She placed it in George's inbox on Monday atop a growing stack of papers. *Where is he today?* she wondered. He hadn't been spotted since the day she met him in the holding room. *Probably off being important.*

On Thanksgiving Day, she discovered his whereabouts, by chance, while mashing potatoes.

"Your boss is on TV," said her mother while prepping the green bean casserole.

"He's on TV every day," said Hope. She felt a tug on her apron. "I've seen the commercials."

Lucas, her five-year-old nephew stood at Hope's side and probed her face with big brown eyes. "Auntie Hope?"

She picked him up and set him on the counter, wiped her hands and pressed down his cowlick. "What is it sweetie?"

Lines of concern crossed his forehead. "Is today the day we eat pie?"

Hope laughed. "I never thought of it like that, but yes, Mr. Lucas, today we ..."

"You're missing it," her mother interjected. "Would it kill you to look at the TV? He's in the parade. Right in front of Macy's."

Hope turned just in time to see George blowing kisses from a red-lettered Love by George float. He wore a black tux and was surrounded by models in princess costumes.

Her mother swooned. "I bet those lips taste lovely."

"Mother! Stop being disgusting in front of your grandson."

"There's nothing disgusting about it. Are you blind? Look at him."

Lucas whispered, "What's he like in real life, Auntie?"

"Almost as handsome as you," said Hope, suddenly wondering, *How does someone like George spend Thanksgiving? The family turkey thing? Hard to imagine.*

It wasn't until the next day that the concept of family crossed George's mind that weekend. Having just bagged and tagged a quartzite rock from Mount Wheeler, New Mexico's highest peak, he packed his gear into an SUV in the Taos Ski Valley parking lot. A minivan pulled up alongside him and sputtered to a stop. The door slid open.

"I don't *want* to go, daddy," whined a tiny voice. A auburn-headed girl turned and faced the back seat and clung to it. "I want to see how it ends."

"This is the last bathroom for miles, honey," said her father. "You should try to go. Think of it as a pre-emptive strike. You can watch the end of your movie after we take care of business, okay?" He picked her up and hoisted her onto his shoulders. The girl's mother joined them and squeezed her daughter's hand.

"But I want to know what happens *now*," objected the girl.

"What do you think happens?" asked her father. "Don't princesses always marry princes?"

"And live happily ever after like you and mommy?"

He laughed and set her feet on the ground. "See? You know how it ends." He brushed the hair from his wife's eyes, tucked it behind her ear and kissed her lips slowly. Then, he bent down and raspberried his daughter's neck until she giggled.

Of all places. Out here in the middle of nowhere, thought George, marveling at what the industry referred to as "the real deal," or at least a potential real deal. More study would have been required to verify its authenticity, but not much. He tried recalling when he last witnessed it – a marriage the way it ought to be, long after the honeymoon ended. *Two years ago? Three?* By his count, at least 99 out of 100 couples never experienced lasting fulfillment. On the rare occasion that he stumbled across the phenomenon, he took feverish notes, hoping to pinpoint the intangible that eluded the masses. When asked about their relationship, real-deal couples always said the same thing: You just know.

George had never "just known," not personally. Occasionally, he toyed with the idea of pursuing his own real deal. *After I sell the business,* he promised himself. *Just another year or two. What's the rush? I'm not even 35 years old.* For now, if he could identify and bottle up the real deal, he could sell it to clients and add another zero to his net worth. But if that didn't happen, retirement would be within reach soon enough. Then he could disappear on his yacht and figure out what came next.

As he accelerated out of the parking lot, the image of the minivan family remained fresh. He had planned on using the windshield time to rehearse voice inflections for his upcoming commercial. There were at least ten ways to say "Hi, I'm George Springs" and "Love by George." But the words "happily ever after like you and mommy" rattled the echo chamber in his skull. A patch of black ice soon silenced it.

In the split second it took George to let off the gas pedal, it was already too late. The vehicle fishtailed around the curb at 45 miles an hour. He steered then counter steered. Ice thrust the SUV across the median – within inches of an oncoming semi-truck. Turned backward now, the vehicle careened off the pavement into pine trees and clusters of boulders.

He was going to crash.

Glass shattered. The roof pressed down on George's head when the vehicle flipped. Then it yanked his body sideways, stressing the muscles in his side and neck. *I'm dreaming,* he thought, dazed. Then the airbag deployed, forcing breath from his lungs. Before flipping again, the SUV slammed into a tree and teetered to a stop. With waning consciousness, George patted his head. *Blood. Not good,* he thought. *Really not good. I'm fine. Fine. Still breathing. Alive. Need to call someone. Ted, Madeline, who else? There is no one else. Can't reach my phone. I'll just ... close my ... eyes.*

Darkness.

Chapter 9

"The hospital said *what?*" barked Ted into his phone. "Oh, *I know* how convincing doctors sound. The last one I saw charged me three hundred bucks for telling me to go home and eat chicken noodle soup. Had to go back again two days later. Finally, that quack checked my ears and saw the infection. Forget what the hospital told you, Madeline. I already booked the 6 a.m. flight to Taos. I'll give you an *honest* assessment of George's condition tomorrow."

The next morning, he bought the *Journal* before boarding his flight. *The usual crap,* he thought, scouring the financials after taking his seat and buckling in: real estate foreclosures, gold speculation, insider trading rumors. As the plane reached cruising altitude, he perused the remaining headlines. *Isn't there ANY news today?* he thought. He tossed the paper onto the seat beside him, adequately informed: light trading on Wall Street, 1.6 trillion shares expected to be traded. Black Friday sales projections did not impress.

He took his in-flight coffee black, no cream or sugar. Real coffee. He craved peanuts. *Can't have those now, can we?* he thought. *Might kill someone with allergies. Lawsuits over peanuts. Hal would like that. What a world this is.*

The flight attendant appeared with a bowl of melon. He poked at it with a fork. His own words from a month ago now replayed in his mind: "Of course, you're going to the parade," he told George, who had offered to spend the day with him instead. "Don't be a fool. Lucy wants me all to herself anyway. You can't miss the Macy's Thanksgiving Day Parade!" *Sell it, Ted, you wuss,* he remembered thinking at the time. Lucy, his dog, wasn't the strongest excuse. Had his inner wuss spoken – though the ex-marine in him would never allow it – he could have prevented the reality now facing him. *Don't go, George,* he tried to picture himself saying. *I need company. Every time I stare at Ellie's chair, I lose an hour. Why her? Why not me?*

Turbulence brought him back to the present. Two rows back, a voice uttered the words "life coach" – words Ted usually pounced on. "My life coach is Dr. Kevorkian," he would jeer back. Today it wasn't funny. "God, please fix him," he mouthed instead, staring out the window. George was unconscious in a hospital.

Five years ago, Ellie, Ted's wife, had passed. Cancer. Cells behaving badly, he had jokingly called it when she was first diagnosed, when the oncologist sounded hopeful. Since her death, George had insisted on babysitting Ted on every holiday. Except this one. After the Macy's parade, Ted watched the early football game, but lasted only until halftime. Restless, he drove to the cemetery, rolled down the window of his Mercedes and stared at his wife's headstone. Snow pelted his face, stinging and melting, a sensation reminding him that he was alive and she was not. The world was worse off because of it. Lucy napped for the better part of an hour in the passenger seat before whimpering and cocking her terrier head. "I miss her too, girl," said Ted. He scratched her ears and gave her a Milk-bone, then fired the ignition.

The following day, Black Friday, he returned. After grieving another hour, he headed home and parked in front of the "Go Away. Really." sign on his garage door. He loved that sign – its practicality, the way it got right to the point and didn't sugarcoat its intent. It repelled the neighborhood and solicitors alike. He stared at the words now, thinking about the lifetime of memories inside his empty house. A Manhattan on the rocks would've made him feel something other than numbness. Perhaps. He slouched down in the seat, flipped open his cell phone and retrieved the only archived message: the one he still listened to every day.

"Love you, Teddy," said Ellie's ailing voice on her last good day. "Not a single day has gone by in the past 30 years that I haven't been grateful for you coming into my life. Don't you forget it, my big, strong man. The doctor says it won't be long now. Do me a favor? Hold onto the good times. All of them. There are so many. You won't have time to be sad if you do that. I'll be in a better place, waiting for you." She blew a kiss and hung up.

He played the message again, longing to hold her again. To tell her everything that mattered. To hear her say words like "dirt!" – something she said instead of cursing – and "Manhattan," which she enunciated like a native New Yorker – "Mun-*hat*-un."

Suddenly, his phone rang. "Unknown Number" appeared on the display screen. *Telemarketer?* he wondered. *On the day after Thanksgiving? Bet I can make you wish you were never born.* "Hello?"

"Mr. Theodore Marble please."

"Speaking."

The caller introduced himself as the lead physician at a hospital in Taos and explained that George was under his care. "Not good, I'm afraid," he said. "He arrived unconscious. I'm running tests for hemorrhaging and cracked ribs. I'm guessing that he'll snap out of this at some point. Probably best for him to see a familiar face when he does. I can't promise he'll be the same. The effects of head trauma are unpredictable. We found your name on an emergency contact card in his wallet."

The doctor's words haunted Ted now, until the flight attendant's voice again filled the cabin:

"Ladies and gentlemen, the pilot has turned on the fasten seat belt sign. We are now making our final descent into Taos. Please fasten your seat belts, return your seats and tray tables to the upright position and turn off all portable electronic devices."

Final approach? thought Ted. *Where did two hours go? What hospital was it again? There can't be more than one in this tumbleweed town. Holy something or another.*

"Ted? I thought that was you. Lucky bumping into you again after all these years," said a passenger across the aisle. He wore a bomber jacket and had salt-and-pepper hair feathered back over his ears. "I never forget a brother."

"Were we in combat together?"

"No, but I did pull the trigger on a stock tip you gave me years ago. Guess that makes us Wall Street Brothers."

"We've met? Uh, ..."

"Brian." He extended his hand. They shook. "You don't remember me? The conference at the Wolstein Center?"

Ted bulged his eyes. "Well, crap! There goes my photographic memory."

"Forgot Cleveland, huh? Well, it's not exactly Huntington Beach. There's Lake Eerie, I guess, if you can stomach the smell. Definitely not on the conference A-list. If memory serves, I think we were supposed to meet in San Antonio, but it was booked. So we got Cleveland. Anyway, I just wanted to say hello. You seemed preoccupied earlier. I didn't want to bother you."

"I appreciate that. Bothering people is my job. I'm better at it than anyone I know."

When the plane landed and finished taxiing, he shoved past everyone ahead of him. "Emergency!" he exclaimed. "Doctor coming through."

Minutes later, he peeled out of the parking lot in a rental sedan. *What if he doesn't remember anything?* he worried. *How do I jog his memory? Stock market stories? No shortage of those. Alaska fishing trip – the attack of the No See Um bugs? Naw. He'll probably start flailing and bonk his head again. A college flashback?*

In three short years after graduating, George had turned thousands into millions in the stock market. He funneled profits into his new venture, Love by George, a matchmaking startup, a sole proprietorship. His future plans were no secret: going public, turning LBG into a Fortune 500 Company, then disappearing at sea. He was now close, Ted knew, and so much more refined than in his youth. No one acquainted with George now would believe him capable of his former pranks – like removing the bell from atop a Taco Bell restaurant with his college roomies and depositing it two blocks away in a rival frat house's front yard.

That works, thought Ted as he burst through the hospital's sliding glass doors. *The Taco Bell heist. If he remembers that, he's fine.* "I'm here to see George Springs," he told the receptionist, thumping his hand down on the counter.

"Now that's funny," she said, twirling her scarf, looking over his shoulder.

"Pardon me?"

She pointed to a boy and a girl tussling over a nativity set.

"Mine!" shouted the boy.

"No, mine!" the girl snapped, tearing a figurine from his grasp.

"Enough!" said a man, presumably their father. "Fighting over the baby Jesus this close to Christmas? Do you have any idea how wrong this is?"

"Yeah. Whatever," said Ted. "Look, I'm here to see ..."

"Awww," cooed the receptionist. "He traded baby Jesus for the ox and the lamb. How sweet is that?"

"And who do I trade you for? I need to see George Springs! If you can't make it happen, find me someone who can."

Wide-eyed, she requested his ID. Comparing it to his face, she scowled and buzzed open the door, then led him down a hallway that reeked of antiseptic. "Here we are," she said, stopping at Room 221. "Try not to *disturb ...*"

Ted brushed her aside. After shutting the door, he surveyed the room: A monitor beeped. George's chest rose and fell. His upper body was slightly propped up. Pillows had been shoved against the bed rails, cushioning his ribs. His head was wrapped in gauze – three or four times around, underneath his chin to the top of his head. Only a trace of color in his face, which was mostly unscathed. Only one minor scratch on his forehead.

He grabbed George's hand – neither warm nor cold – and pulled up a chair. Flashbacks of Ellie's last days flooded him. The hospital had assigned her numbers for alertness. A x O x 3 they would say on good days – alert and oriented times three: aware of who she was, where she was and what time it was. Her last A x O x 3 was two weeks before her passing – the day that she left him the voicemail, the day that her hand last caressed his cheek. She looked better then than George did now. *Definitely an A x O x zero,* he thought. *Maybe if he hears my voice.*

Ted unfolded his newspaper and read the first headline aloud. "WOBBLER, BATTERY PARK'S FEARLESS NOMAD." He cleared his throat. "While frolicking through Battery Park yesterday, 4-year-old Meredith Austen of Seattle stooped down and went nose to beak with Battery Park's celebrity. Wobbler, a wild turkey that has become a park fixture, paused from grousing for foliage ... Foliage?" questioned Ted, glancing at George. "Don't birds eat worms and bird seed? Whatever! Anyway ... Meredith begged her mother to take a picture and post it on Facebook. 'He's posing for us, momma,' she said." Ted guffawed. "Posing turkeys? Rrright. Maybe when they are dead and stuffed and coming out of the oven. And a 4-year-old on Facebook? Sick and wrong, Georgie. Let's try NO COMMENT FROM GOVERNOR RE: CASINO DEALINGS instead. Ten to one, there isn't a word in here about hush money. Hard to find truth in print these days. It's not like reporting is rocket science. All you have to do is follow the money." It took Ted some time to read through the paper and insert his commentary in this manner. Yawning overtook him by the time he finished.

"Think I'll shut my eyes too for a while if you don't mind," he said, stretching. "Where's your doctor? Why hasn't he stopped in? Doesn't matter, I guess. I'm here now. Everything's going to be fine." He reclined his chair against the wall and drifted away.

An hour later, his mouth twitched. Agitated into semi-consciousness, he scratched it without opening his eyes and felt something warm and sticky.

"I can't believe that you came all this way to see me," said a familiar voice. "You've helped me make a crucial discovery. Hospital food *is* good for something."

"Whaaa ?" said Ted, startled. George's eyes were open and animated. He was A x O x 3: sitting and sucking applesauce from his finger. He had filled Ted's right hand with it then tickled his mouth. Itching, Ted smeared applesauce all over his face. "Give me that napkin before I knock you back into La La Land. And if you ever scare me like that again …."

"This is all your fault," said George, examining the bandages on his ribs. "I offered to spend Thanksgiving with you, but you prefer the company of that mutt."

Ted grunted. "Yeah, well, at least Lucy doesn't …"

The door swung open, and in walked the doctor – bearded, portly, a horrendous comb-over. He clutched a clipboard. "Still with us," he said, eyeballing his patient. "That's a good sign." He shined a pen light in George's eyes and checked his breathing (he had done this half an hour ago while Ted slept). "Lucky you didn't fracture those ribs. Just severe bruising. Even so, like I said, you'll probably experience some lingering pain. All this over a rock, you say?"

"Tell me about it," Ted chimed in. "You can't kill yourself collecting stamps or …."

"How much did he pay you to tee that up for him, doc?" interrupted George, rolling his eyes.

"We hadn't discussed compensation, but I like where this is headed. Big breath now." He placed the stethoscope bell on George's back. "Your pain level – zero to ten?"

"Not too bad," said George. "Maybe a three."

"When those pain-killers wear off, you'll feel it more. I'll have another look at you in the morning and probably sign your release. Unless something changes. So don't go changing on me.

No reading tonight. TV is okay. And unless you need to use the bathroom, stay in bed."

The only overnight change was in Ted's anxiety level. It dissipated after George sailed through the Taco Bell test. Furthermore, nothing prevented the doctor from releasing George the next morning.

After their plane touched down at O'Hare in the early afternoon, the two shared a taxi home. Ted instructed the cab driver to wait as he escorted George indoors.

"Easy does it," said Ted, seeing his boss to the living room couch. He fetched a blanket and heating pad, and placed his cell phone and several bottles of water on the coffee table in front of him. "I'll call you in a couple of hours. Try not to off yourself again before then, okay? Oh, and don't worry about breakfast. I'll round something up in the morning."

George stood and stepped gingerly. "I'm fine. See? Stop your fussing."

His feebleness aroused Ted's inner wuss again. Eyes watering, he embraced George head-on, mano-a-mano. "Just – let me do this."

"I'm fine, Ted. Really."

"Of course you are. Now get your butt back on that couch. And pick up the phone when I call," his voice sputtered as he marched off. After shutting the front door, he whispered, "You're all I got, kid."

Chapter 10

Paige Walker nosed down at the empty chair behind the Love by George front desk. The open sign in the front window had been turned on, but Karli's seat was vacant. The only employee in sight was Hope. She perused the file cabinet, her back toward Paige.

"Uh, yoo-hoo? Miss?" Paige called out, snapping her fingers. "Sorry to interrupt *whatever* it is you are doing there. I'm sure it's important. I have a 9 o'clock with George."

"George?" repeated Hope, turning. "I don't think he's in today. I'll check with Karli. She's just in the ...."

"You *are* capable of picking up the phone, aren't you?" interrupted Paige. "How about knocking on his door? Think you can handle that? Oh, never mind. Just get me Carla or whatever her name is, you know, the professional. And be quick about it. I don't have all morning." She shook her head and muttered to the camera man behind her, "The help around here gets more incompetent all the time, and shorter."

Before Hope – all 5'2 of her – could respond, Karli returned, apologizing for the inconvenience, which only fueled Paige's condescension. The visitors strode down the executive wing with an air of self-importance.

"Now you tell me," said Liz, emerging from her cubicle. "*What* could George possibly see in that? Except curves. Then she opens her mouth, and you sort of lose that."

"*That's* George's girlfriend?" marveled Hope. "I can't believe that he would show up today after what he's been through, *especially for that.* Madeline must have forgotten to cancel his appointments." Like the rest of the minions, all weekend long,

Hope had kept vigil, monitoring the 24-hour news coverage of George's accident – tidbits from ambulance chasers and eyewitnesses, and images of his mangled vehicle. George's present condition remained a question mark.

"Did you see his SUV?" Liz let out a low whistle.

"Rough weekend," said Hope. "Mary said that Ted went down and got him, and escorted him back to Chicago yesterday."

As if on cue, the front door opened, and George stepped through it. He glided across the lobby – coffee in one hand, a thumbs up gesture and flashed his signature smile.

"George?" said Liz, straightening up. "Were your ears ringing? We were just talking about you. We were all sick with worry, but look at you."

"Worrying is bad for the complexion," replied George. He checked his watch. "Can't believe everything you see on TV. No time to chat. I'm late."

He turned down the executive wing. "Give me five minutes," he said, poking his head in Madeline's doorway. Upon reaching his office, he shut the door and collapsed in a chair. *Thank God for painkillers,* he thought. The moments ahead called for a show of strength. For once, he needed Paige. She could record his prepared statement as well as anyone, he reasoned. She was a known quantity, safer than a stranger.

"Want the exclusive?" he had asked her over the phone the previous night. "My office. Tomorrow morning, say nine-ish? And see if you can round up a camera. Looks like the TV stations are desperate for filler material. I bet some might even broadcast factual information if given the chance."

"Of course," said Paige. "I'm always here for you, Georgie."

Predictably, she monopolized the camera instead of turning the lens on him during the interview and prodding like a normal reporter. He maintained a sturdy voice throughout, extinguishing the media's conjecture of his compromised state.

He left the office minutes later and phoned Ted from his Porche. "I'm not quite 100 percent," he said. "My pain pill is wearing off. Do me a favor? Fill in for the coffee run? I need to go lay down."

"I can't believe you showed up here today," Ted replied. "Actually, yes I can. I almost hunted you down and grabbed you by the lapels. Go home. I got this."

No one objected to the substitution, despite it being Ted's virgin coffee run. To date, he had always declined, scoffing at what a waste five-dollar coffee was. But it was George's only request. So Madeline prepared Ted a cheat sheet. "Put all the drinks on my tab," he told the cashier. After everyone ordered, he lowered his voice and unfolded his paper. "And, uh, give me a tall, which I'm told is really a small, uh, Americano with, uh, strike that, I mean without room."

"You mean no room?" asked the cashier.

"Do I look like I know what I mean? Who talks like this? I'm no coffee snob. Just give me coffee. No cream. No sugar. No baloney."

The next day, George lasted at the office until noon. On his way out, he delegated the coffee run again. And so Marbles got his second taste of the good stuff. The extra shot of espresso transformed him into a regular chatterbox. "Tell me something, Burt," he cajoled. "Did you go out on maneuvers over the weekend again with that new gadget of yours?"

Burt, the IT monkey, spent weekends with his GPS, geo-caching in the middle of nowhere for buried rubbish. "... it was touch and go there," he replied, providing a play-by-play of the wood tick ambush in the sticks of Tennessee. He rolled up his sleeves and revealed a smattering of dots on his forearms.

"Little hickeys of near-death by the look of them," chortled Ted.

Burt's eyes blazed.

Aware that he had offended, Ted grabbed Burt's cup and returned to the coffee line. *It's the caffeine talking*, he thought. *All natural thoughts when you think about it. If you want polite conversation, Burt, maybe you should GPS on over to the tea and crumpets shop.*

Ninety minutes later, the caffeine relinquished its hold. *Cripes!* thought Ted, slipping out of the office for his first three-a-day. *What have I become?*

His craving compounded yet again the next day, a troubling development for a control freak. After his fourth Americano (two during the coffee run, two more after sneaking out under the guise of appointments), he could no longer steady his hands. More troubling still was George's behavior. That morning, George shut his office door. He opened it only to pay for a boxed lunch and ignored all emails. *What is he doing in there?* wondered Ted, pausing at George's door before leaving that evening. There was only silence.

George continued his confinement and did not break pattern the remainder of the week or the beginning of the next. Then, one afternoon, he summoned Abby – who coordinated commercial campaigns – to his office. Half an hour later, she emerged teary-eyed, announcing her immediate retirement.

"Are you out of your mind?" growled Ted, barging into George's office. "How could you let her go?"

"How could I not?" said George. "Since when do my decisions require approval? I sort of own the company. Look, you know Abby: She's been talking about someday for years. Someday I'll retire. Someday I'll spend time with my grandkids. Translation: someday, I'll live. You get one life, Ted. One! It's the ultimate deadline. It's wrong to let someday slip through your fingers. I just helped Abby realize that."

Ted fumed. "Well it sounds like we've made *all kinds of progress* here today. Who died and made you shrink? Tell me: Who is going to fill her shoes?"

"Hmmm. Hadn't thought of that."

"Obviously!" snapped Ted, looking around. He pointed to an easel turned backward in front of the windows.

"What is that?"

"Nothing."

Ted walked over and flipped it around. It was a canvas depicting a yacht struggling against a tilted sea of whitecaps and wind and gloom. He touched the corner of the frame and rubbed his fingers together. "Painting? I thought you hung that up in college."

"The urge struck again."

"A bit dark for you, isn't it?"

"Something I dreamed, actually."

Ted shook his head and left. "Keep an eye on him," he ordered Madeline in the hallway. "He's painting his nightmares in there. No explanation for releasing Abby. Can you believe it? Two weeks before the new commercial shoot. So much for bouncing things off us first. We'll have to postpone until we find a new Abby."

Madeline shook her head. "Not happening. You know him. He insists on staying on schedule. I guess I could place a help wanted ad in the *Tribune*."

"There's no time for that," said Ted. "We can't put him on that plane alone. Not in his condition. I'd babysit him myself if I knew anything about advertising."

"What about Hope? You know how he brags about her." Hope's reports were, in fact, the lone work-related task that George had taken interest in since his accident. He frequently boasted of them in emails. In seven short weeks, Hope had taken a troop of lost causes and landed third dates for ten of them, squeezing more out of social media than anyone thought possible. So impressed was George, that two weeks before Taos, he encouraged employees that did not have a social media account to create one. Work deadlines still came first, he stressed, but he gave the green light for social networking during breaks. The suggestion scored points with the rank and file. Only Ted objected.

"Total waste of company time," he said, reluctantly agreeing to try it out before passing final judgment. Several days later, he buzzed George's office phone, asking, "And just *what* am I supposed to do with a virtual poke?"

"I don't know," said George. "Poke back?"

"If it were a guy, I'd clock him. Only it's not."

"Oh? Anyone I know?"

"High school classmate. By the look of her, she's taking vinegar for a daily suppliment. Anyway, this poking business, does it mean, you know …. Do you think she's got the hots for me? I can just hear it now: Same old Ted. Too stuck up to ask me to prom. Now he won't return my virtual poke."

George chuckled. "Just be yourself. It always makes for interesting conversation."

"Thanks for nothing. I hate Facebook."

Several days later, Ted recanted. "The social media thing, lame as it is, has a certain appeal to the juvenile," he told George in a flat voice. "But that's a big chunk of our clientele, so I guess it would be unwise not to leverage it. Take that as my endorsement. I knew Hope had potential, you know. She was my hire."

Maybe she could handle the commercials, thought Ted, now that Madeline planted the seed. *She's proven. She has the background. SOMEONE has to keep an eye on George.* Ted burst in on George again, this time with Madeline, demanding the substitution.

"I can't do that to her," objected George. "Not on such short notice. Not over the Holidays."

Ted and Madeline pressed.

Minutes later, they convened in the executive conference room and summoned Hope. Ted motioned for her to enter when she appeared in the doorway. "Ever think about making *You're Welcome* cards?" he asked. "You know, a response to a *Thank You* card. Of course, then you'd need a *Thank You* card for the *You're Welcome* card. There's got to be a gold mine in all that back and forth. Or better yet, *No Thank You* cards. I can't tell you how many gifts I'd like to return with a *No Thank You* card."

"This is why you called me?" asked Hope, glancing at Madeline, then George. "To discuss greeting cards? I don't think you want to go there again."

"So perceptive," said Ted, "and such a lovely dress. Why you've brightened the room by stepping into it." Burgundy and shimmery, with intricate ruching and striated straps, the dress wrapped Hope's frame in a cotton-poly hug. It was the dress she would have worn to the company Christmas party if she had a date.

YOU noticed my dress? thought Hope. *YOU of all people! You are the only person who said anything about it all day.*

After urging her to sit, Ted explained the dilemma of Abby's retirement and how they needed someone who knew the ins and outs of commercial advertising to fill in.

"Feel free to say no," said George. "I assume that you have already made holiday plans."

"Plans?" repeated Hope. "Pffft. Before I had distractions. *Now* I have plans. When do we leave?" *A jaunt to the West Coast?* she thought, her mind racing ahead to the itinerary. *Pinch me! I could use a break from this cold. Plus a chance to prove myself. And maybe a night or two out on the town with the boss?*

Madeline cracked open her planner and relayed flight options.

Flying! thought Hope. *Of course you'll be flying, you idiot. LA isn't a two-hour road trip. How could you forget about the flying? Next time, why not just say, "Choose me! Choose me! I want to die."* Elevator rides were a picnic in comparison. Elevators got stuck. Planes crashed. Over the next two weeks, sleep abandoned Hope. Her waking thoughts turned morbid. The only mental reprieve she had during the entire fortnight prior to her departure came the day before Christmas Eve.

That morning, George led a skeleton crew to the coffee shop, his first run since the accident. After ordering, he asked Mary, "What's going in the garden next spring?" and followed it up with a sincere "Has your boy conquered algebra yet?" Then he urged Liz to opine on the latest political developments – a 10-minute soapbox everyone avoided.

What is he doing? everyone wondered. Gone was George's familiar habit of breaking eye contact within seconds of asking a question – a mannerism which always struck employees as though he wished to be recognized for thoughtful inquiry and nothing more, a man who heard every third word of an answer. Not today. Today, he was all tuned in, but why? Was it holiday cheer? The accident? Something else?

After a full 15 minutes of this behavior, he lapsed into silence. His eyes drifted – to the coffee line, to the front door, to adjacent tables – before settling on Hope for a second longer than she was prepared for. Then he winked and smiled. It triggered an immediate bout of coughing and sputtering in Hope.

"I'm fine," she said, raising a hand. "Just forgot how to swallow."

The phone was ringing when Hope returned to her office – her mother calling with the daily horoscope: "*Today* is a nine!" she chirped. "Try as you may to focus on the task ahead, but fate has other plans. Did you hear that, Hope? Today is your nine! Today you don't have to think. Fate has your back."

"I can hardly contain myself. It's *just* a number."

"Six is just a number. Seven is just a number. Nine is a sign. Nines should be seized, not questioned, especially nines about fate. Today could be the day you meet *him*."

"Yes. How nice for him. He's already got a burial plot. And what if he doesn't exist? Ever ask yourself that?"

Another tongue-lashing followed until her mother changed the topic to the holiday schedule – The Nutcracker, midnight mass, exchanging gifts, morning coffee and rolls on Christmas Day, brunch afterward. She ended the conversation with, "Fine. Throw away your nine. Just don't forget to bring dessert."

The nine came up repeatedly over the next 48 hours – twice during The Nutcracker, again at midnight mass and once more as they prepared Christmas brunch. "Mother!" said Hope. "Let it go! For God's sake, it's Christmas."

Her mother responded by nitpicking over the ham that Hope was slicing. "Follow the muscle line!" she ordered in a sharp voice, waving the instruction manual in front of Hope's face. "Like so!"

"It's pre-sliced, Mother. There's no wrong way to do this."

"Just give me that!" She sliced the rest of the ham in accordance with the manual. In solitude. Nothing cleared a room as fast as her mother's perfectionism.

To Hope's annoyance, the properly cut slices tasted better. Most days, Hope tolerated her mother with secret regard. There was a certain Socratic, albeit grating beauty to her – the way that she chased what others thought out of reach, the way she knew that she needed her husband to balance her and the unapologetic way that she spoke her mind because she knew she was right. Hope recognized some of the same perfectionistic tendencies within herself, sometimes resenting them, sometimes embracing them. Were they strengths or weaknesses? Maybe both. All too often, life's struggles revealed troubling flaws. But sometimes they yielded something better. Like now. After all the fuss, her mother had a perfect Christmas ham. Just like sometimes Hope found the perfect words.

Eventually, her mother's tone returned to normal. "Better take something to help you sleep tonight, honey," she said. "You know how you get with airplanes."

I barely survived the ham, thought Hope. *Tomorrow, at least there's something to look forward to. I can lose myself in George's eyes as we plummet to our deaths – after we properly affix our oxygen masks. Probably best that way. Zero chance of choking on that smile again if it's covered up. Of course, he probably won't be smiling – a tragedy upon a tragedy now that I think about it. Such a smile! Will he hold my hand if we crash? That would be nice. And I'd still have his eyes. Unless he winks again and it stops my breathing.*

Pie followed brunch, silencing talk of airplanes. Next, they watched *It's a Wonderful Life*. Then came the second round of Honey Baked ham and mashed potatoes, and hearing about the nine again. Then more pie, the annual game of Monopoly, and finally, well into the night, sangria around the Christmas tree before Hope departed.

During the drive home, clouds veiled the half moon. Hope couldn't stop yawning as she sped down the Interstate. It was late. But what did it matter? *I can crash tomorrow,* she thought. *Literally.* Already packed, she flopped onto her bed when she arrived home.

If she dreamed, she awakened with no memory of it. Three hours before takeoff, she pulled into the parking lot of a coffee shop just a few miles from the airport. *The Last Coffee?* she thought, reading the storefront sign. *Appropriately named.* She scanned the lot for April's car. *Late as usual.*

Hope texted: *they won't delay my flight 4 u, girl. killer line here. ordering your latte.*

sorry, b there soon, April replied. *vinny's gone missing.*

Only in your world, Apes, thought Hope. *How can a snake be a priority?* She grabbed the newspaper in her handbag and flipped to the horoscope. "Today is a four," it read. "Storm clouds follow you. Unwillingness to change plans could be your downfall. One wrong turn and you will wish that you had never gotten out of bed."

"Your order, ma'am?" asked the barista.

Hope heard nothing. Not after seeing her horoscope. In essence, a four was a zero – the lowest possible rating. Newspapers never doled out ones, twos or threes. Mayhem would result. Readers would fear the falling sky. They wouldn't venture outdoors. Only on the rarest of occasions did newspapers drop a four. On any other day, Hope would have laughed it off. *Could* have laughed it off. Not today. Today four was confirmation. Four was gospel. *What else can it possibly mean except death by airplane?* she thought.

"Ma'am?" repeated the barista, projecting her nasally voice.

Hope ordered drinks and scones and found a swivel chair in front of the window. Between cowering sips, as airplanes flew overhead, she fixated on the words "storm clouds follow you," "change plans" and "your downfall."

"Carpe California," April said when she arrived. Shedding a coat, she sat.

"Any luck finding Vinny?" asked Hope.

"Not yet. He'll turn up. What about you? Get any sleep?"

"Why sleep? I'm just going to crash right after takeoff." Hope slid April's latte across the table. Through the windows, she watched pigeons peck at sidewalk crumbs. Snow began to fall.

"You know, flying is safer than …," said April.

"Don't! Three hours from now, after the crash, when they cut open passengers to identify their remains, tell them I'm the one with the half-digested cranberry orange scone in her stomach."

April rolled her eyes. "You worry too much."

"What did you expect - hitting *The Last Coffee* before takeoff? Good call."

"It's just a name. Clever marketing, actually. You of all people should appreciate that. Besides, it's snowy, not icy. The runways will be fine."

"Or ridden with storm clouds, downfalls and wrong turns."

"What are you talking about?" asked April

"A horoscope four."

"You've been spending too much time with your mother. Just text me when you land."

"I can't text from a fetal ball. Let's just hit the word list, *the last* word list." Hope clicked her pen and assumed the writing position.

"Squalor," April began, pausing for Hope to jot it down. "Fraught with possibility." She offered up ten more words and phrases before ending with "plaything."

"I could use a new plaything," said Hope. "*The last*

plaything."

"Especially one with blue eyes, since green turned out to be such a waste. Speaking of which, what's Blue Eyes up to in Dreamland these days?"

"No idea." Hope opened her dream journal. There were no new entries.

"No dreams? That's weird. You always dream."

Hope shrugged. "Maybe I dreamed *the last* dream."

"Could be a neural connectivity issue or ...." April turned the page and stopped. "What's this?"

"Not a dream."

April read it aloud:

> *"An untucked feeling, quickly repressed –*
> *with whys, not nows, maybe nevers,*
> *while Pandora bangs on her box*
> *of unspoken truths, of unconnected dots,*
> *just reining it in again and again."*

"Now we're talking!" said April. "And what's *his* name?"

"Him who? There is no him."

"Then what's untucked feelings about?"

"Just playing with words. Words are my playthings. Oh look." Hope pointed out the window. A blue bird had swooped down, scattering the pigeons. It hopped along, twitching its head back and forth in the flurries. "Never seen that before in the city."

"And me without my good camera," said April, snapping a photo with her cell phone. "A bluebird is a good omen: It can mean joy, ecstasy, love or ...."

"Or *the last* bluebird for some of us." Hope shoved her notebook into her handbag.

"Hey. You're gonna' be fine. Okay? Just focus on your new plaything, Mr. Tucked Feelings."

"Mr. I-Have-No-Idea-What-You're-Talking-About for the last time."

"Fine. No tucked feelings. No airplane talk. Anything else?"

"Untucked," said Hope.

Covering a smirk, April sipped her latte.

Hope stared out the window again and rubbed the Celtic charm that Mac, the elevator attendant, had loaned her. "For luck," he had said when he presented it the day Hope agreed to the LA trip. "It won't fail ye. It has kept me safe in all me travels. Return it when ye come back. We'll take a quick dash to the top of the Cock then. Celebrate good and proper."

Or not! thought Hope, watching the blue bird fly off. *On such a dreary day, why not just cozy up in your nest? Why go anywhere at all?* The reflection cued the words that still haunted: "One wrong turn and you may wish that you had never gotten out of bed." *Just try not to make a boob of yourself again in front of George. That's what your horoscope should have said.*

Chapter 11

There are pills for air travel. Pop a couple and all feeling ceases. But what's a poet minus feelings, especially despair? Pills were a last resort for Hope. She took an aspirin once, maybe twice a year, when headaches couldn't be slept off or bubble bathed into remission. "You only have one liver," she argued when doctors pushed prescription drugs. "I'm saving mine for the nursing home years."

Dodging pills was one thing. Dodging pathogens at O'Hare quite another. When Hope passed through security, the ticketing agent – after dabbing his bulbous nose with a handkerchief – examined her driver's license and boarding pass without gloves. *Bare handed!* she thought. *What is this, the Dark Ages?* A second wave of germs assailed her at the stack of personal effects trays. *When were these last disinfected? Why isn't there a time stamp?* She picked up two with her fingertips, one for her laptop, one for everything else and felt violated by the way that the security guard eyeballed her. *Stop staring at me like I'm the underwear bomber. I feel naked enough without my wristwatch.*

After putting on her jewelry, belt and shoes again, she scurried off toward Gate C14. *White knuckles in T-minus one hour,* she thought, now studying the arrival-departure monitors. Her phone vibrated.

found vinny! April's text read. *he slithered back on top of his cage. he's sooo cold. we r snuggling n bed.*

"Ewww," said Hope, suddenly feeling better about being single, about not sharing her bed with reptiles. She scrolled through her messages and found two unread texts. The first was from her father: *We just lost our Lovergirl.*

Not today, Dad, thought Hope. She checked to see that her

boarding pass was in her handbag, after momentarily freaking that she had left in the security bin. Why did she fret over losing it? It was a first-class death warrant, not the winning Powerball ticket. Her last meal would be half a serving of pretzels, not fine French cuisine.

Checking the monitors again, she watched white-lettered "On Time" statuses turn yellow. Intensifying snowfall sent ticket agents scrambling, announcing delays and cancellations. A chorus of boos sounded at the delay of Flight 7297 to Honolulu. The delay of Fight 6322 to Orlando followed with equal dismay. Flight 6612 to Buffalo, however, was cancelled without fanfare. Approximately a third of all flights, both coming and going, were soon affected by the snowfall. Not Hope's. Flight 4441 nonstop to Los Angeles was tragically on time. *4441,* she thought. *Three fours. The horoscope number.*

She opened the last unread text, surprised to discover it was from George, time stamped 6 p.m. the previous night. *just tried calling u,* it read. *no answer. change of plans. i have 2 take a later flight. will call u when i get 2 LA.* She read it a second time in disbelief, tearing up. *No George? Now I'm going to die all alone. Today IS a four!* She wiped the corner of her eye and felt her shoulder being tapped.

"Everything okay, miss?" asked a woman in a muumuu dress.

"Fine," squeaked Hope, sniffling. "Just wondering why I am here. It's only the quintessential question of life. You would think I would have figured it out by now."

The woman's cracked lips spread into a smile. "There's a reason they sell those tiny bottles of liquor on the airplane, dear. Maybe you can help me. You know, take your mind off things for a bit." She waited for Hope to make eye contact before continuing, then threw back her shoulders. "You look like you know how to pull an outfit together. I'm a little challenged that way, and I need a frank opinion. Do I look alright for a 60-year-old broad?"

"I wouldn't …," said Hope, pausing after seeing the foundation demarcation between the woman's jawbone and neck. It distracted from the gap between her front teeth. *That's got to be worth something*, thought Hope. Then there was the muumuu itself – a splatter of reds, golds and greens. It looked like the woman had somehow survived being at ground zero of a detonated traffic light. "I, uh, wouldn't change a thing. You should get me dolled up sometime."

"Oh go on. You're an awful liar. But look at you! You don't need any tweaking at all, except maybe a splash of red lipstick. Then you'll be perfectly hot." She gazed over Hope's shoulder. "Oh dear!"

"What is it?"

The woman pointed to the window. De-icing crews raced back and forth in trucks as the snowfall thickened. "Looks like someone shook up a snow globe out there," she said. "Oh well. Can't control the weather, I guess. You should put those tears away, dear. He's not worth it."

"He?"

"Yes, he. Those are man tears if I ever saw them. Cried them myself more times than I care to admit. Anyway, thanks again for lying. It needs work though. No time for a makeover now. I'll just have to pull off this outfit with sheer attitude. I better get or I'll miss my flight. Don't forget the red lipstick. Bye now." She hobbled down the terminal.

Red? thought Hope. *I'm in a super-pink pouty mood. And I need to pee.*

O'Hare trafficked 150 million passengers a year, a paralyzing statistic Hope once read. Her mind crunched the numbers now: *150 million passengers. That's 75 million women, give or take. Maybe 30 percent have to go? That's 2.25 million. Twenty ladies rooms at O'Hare? Close enough. What's that - 100,000 a year per bathroom? ... divided by 365 days in a year: about 3,000 per day per ladies room: 6,000 hands, 3,000 bladders, 3,000 colons ... odds of contracting E. Coli, Staphylococcus, Streptococcus, Campylobacter or Salmonella – 12,000 to one. And that's just passengers. What about the pilots? The flight attendants? Airport employees? Peeing here is not safer than flying.* She paused in the entryway. A dishwater blonde scrunched her hair at the sink. *Suck it up, Hope. You can do this.*

She creaked open the stall door second furthest from the entryway. The toilet had been flushed. Exhaling, she backtracked to the sink and set down her coffee cup before returning to the stall. *A seat cover dispenser! How did I not notice that before?* Her eyes descended. The toilet seat appeared spotless in the fluorescent light. But she knew better than to trust it. The remnants of hoverers past – those vile, indiscriminate sprayers that avoid skin contact with porcelain – had to be assumed. Grabbing two sanitizing wipes from her handbag, she scrubbed the seat then tossed the wipes into the toilet. Twice before she had used a seat cover. Both times they had clung to the toilet seat. But why? Had they stuck to the sanitizing wipe residue or stuck to pee that had somehow eluded her wiping? The uncertainty prevented her from using one a third time. Even so, the mere presence of a dispenser provided comfort. Filth *had to be* less pervasive in public stalls with seat cover dispensers, she reasoned, even though for her, bare-cheeked was the only way to go.

Sitting, she goose bumped at the cold of the porcelain until the sound of diarrhea and groaning several stalls away left her feeling all dirty again. Needing an alternate focal point, she did what 91 percent of 28 to 35 year-olds do while indisposed: She reached for her mobile device. She was not one of the 63 percent who, while going, answered incoming calls or made online purchases. She only toilet texted or updated her Facebook status, which she now did: *"Life is like a box of grenades,"* she typed.

After flushing, she washed again and reached for her coffee, then stopped short. *Did I touch that before I washed?* she wondered. She stared at the words on the cup – *"The Last Coffee"* – and searched her memory.

Another blast of diarrhea erupted from the stall behind.

What if SHE touched my cup while I was in the stall? There was no risking it.

"Attention Flight 4441 passengers," a sultry voice announced over the intercom as Hope exited the ladies room. "Your flight with non-stop service from Chicago to Los Angeles has been delayed due to a minor maintenance issue. We are working to resolve the problem as quickly as possible and will keep you posted as more information becomes available."

When Hope arrived at the gate, passengers crowded around the terminal windows, speculating. Runway taxis sped through the falling snow to the jet. "Aren't they going to pop the hood?" one passenger asked. "Why are the mechanics on the ground?"

Are you kidding me? thought Hope. *Some gearhead is going to tighten a couple of lug nuts and release us up into the sky on the same plane? Isn't there an FAA rule preventing this?* She texted April: *flight delayed. "minor" maintenance issue. looks like they r duct taping the engine. don't forget – ½ digested cranberry scone.*

The delay, however, was not entirely without merit. It meant more oxygen. At least for now. Hope celebrated with a fresh macchiato and returned in time for the next update.

"Attention Flight 4441 passengers with non-stop service from Chicago to Los Angeles," the now familiar voice said. "We regret to inform you that the Airbus 300F scheduled to transport you to Los Angeles has a flat tire."

"A flat tire?" the crowd murmured.

"We keep a variety of spare tires on hand," the agent continued, "but this particular one, I am told, is out of stock. We are now in the process of locating a replacement jet. When we do, we will begin boarding the plane as expeditiously as possible. This new flight, however, will not be non-stop. It includes a brief layover in Denver. Please stop by the ticket counter if you have a connecting flight out of LA so we can re-route you. We apologize for the inconvenience."

"Apology accepted," said Hope aloud. *New plane,* she thought. *Take that, universe! Time to rethink your stupid four. One point for Hope.*

The universe responded 90 minutes later. The new jet, a 747, dwarfing the Airbus 300F, taxied to the gate. And the boarding squeeze was on. In haste, passengers were corralled onto the plane. The flight was full, and though the new plane was larger, its size was insufficient to accommodate every first-class passenger. For reasons that were never explained, Hope lost her first-class seat.

To make matters worse, a pheromone-radiating, dread-locked couple boarded in line in front of Hope. The couple stifled the air within a 20-foot radius. After just one waft, Hope updated her Facebook status to: *"Dear couple standing in line in front of me, please shower before boarding the plane. Thank you. Signed, The World."*

It was pointless voicing an olfactory objection to the airline. It smelled only money. It was more inclined to charge extra for the weight of dreadlocks (i.e. the additional jet fuel required to transport them) than it was to enforce hygiene. The agent who punched boarding passes didn't appear to smell anything. He responded to every passenger complaint with "it is what it is."

"Translation: It sucks is what it is," mumbled Hope, crinkling her nose. Losing her seat was the greater offence. Though new to first-class, she turned rather snobbish about almost having a seat there. Coach class suddenly felt beneath her. After all, she was a corporate woman now, earning $90 K a year. Nearly six digits. After checking her bag, she stepped into the cabin and refrained from bracing herself with the seat tops like everyone else did. *How many of you are touching these with unwashed hands?*

She found her place in the cheap seats, 23C. The sight of an unoccupied 23B encouraged her for a moment, spawning hope that the "full flight" announcement was errant. She tucked her handbag beneath 22B after grabbing the last of her sanitizing wipes. *A buffer zone between me and 23A!* she thought. It was almost like being alone, only exciting. Except George wasn't sitting there. Try as she might, she couldn't imagine sitting that close to him. The empty seat suddenly felt emptier. Two seats over, the woman in 23A rested her head on a pillow, dozing against the window. Hope quietly wiped down her surroundings – the armrests, the seat back tray and the smudged in-flight magazine cover. Afterward, she buckled in.

Seconds later, 23B showed up – a 50-something male, greased back hair, muting curry belches with a fist. He fingerprinted every square inch of the armrest, jostling past Hope into his seat. *Did you not just see me wiping that?* thought Hope as he adjusted the reading light and the air gasper.

Flummoxed, she texted April: *about 2 take off. finally! lost my 1st-class seat. & just lost the armrest & my imaginary sanitation bubble. will text u if i survive – after kissing the ground, of course. just got the turn off your cell phone stink eye from the flight attendant. luv u!* Hope squeezed her eyes shut as the plane taxied down the runway.

The 747 reached cruising altitude without incident. A small miracle, Hope thought. Her eyes settled on two men in pilot uniforms sitting across from her.

"Let's *not* do that again," said the closest one. "Although, I have to admit, I have a new respect for Cat 3B runways."

"Roger that." The other tilted his hat over his eyes. "I'd rather plow through a flock of seagulls than try that a second time. Less smoke. Plus all the pretty white feathers. Like Christmas snow."

They chuckled.

"Excuse me," Hope interrupted. "Are you the pilots from the

flight before? You know, the one with the flat tire. How did you get a flat?"

"A two banger, you mean," said the pilot furthest away. "Two flats. The front tires exploded after takeoff. No idea why. Anyway, the rubber got sucked into the engines and smoked them up pretty good. It was a dicey landing, but we managed. Could have been worse."

The other pilot added, "But here's the silver lining: We're on break now until L.A."

Could have been worse? thought Hope. *Tires sucked into the engines? NO idea why? Shouldn't there be an investigation? How do you land with flat tires? I was supposed to be on that plane.* She clutched the arm rests, forgetting about 23B's fingerprints.

"You okay, ma'am?" asked the nearest pilot.

"Fine," squeaked Hope, suddenly aware that her hand was now grasping the filthy arm rest. "Excuse me, I have to go." She unfastened her seat belt and bustled up the aisle.

From the bathroom's dim light, Hope eyed the toilet seat. Fresh out of sanitizing wipes, she straddled the toilet (like those she detested) and hovered. When her bladder relaxed, on the verge of letting loose, turbulence spanked her hips between the wall and sink. The horoscope four was back again. She waited a while, then straddled again when the plane caught a smooth patch. With difficulty, she managed to relieve herself. That's when she noticed the empty toilet paper roll. At least the paper towel dispenser appeared full. But getting a towel meant extending herself toward the sink and chancing a dribble. She stood as still as she could for several seconds, drip drying and wiggled her hips before leaning and reaching toward the dispenser.

What she didn't know, could not have known, was the compromised state of the door's signage. The latch was positioned exactly halfway between the "occupied" and "unoccupied" position. To someone on the outside, the uncertainty of the toilet's availability provided reasonable doubt. Especially if you really had to go.

And so the door swung open just as Hope reached for a paper towel. A pale-skinned, skeleton of a man in suspenders straightened up in the doorway and dropped his jaw.

Hope shrieked.

The skeleton slammed the door.

Trembling, Hope wiped then washed her hands. *I hate you, universe! Now what? I can't stay in here until the plane lands. How am I going to escape this one with dignity? Head down. Walk fast. No eye contact. Get back to your seat as quickly as possible. Picture it. Picture it. Now go!* Inhaling deeply, she swung open the door and stepped into the aisle. She hastened past the gawker and nearly plowed over another.

"Oh!" the second body exclaimed, fumbling with something.

Flecks of sticky liquid pelted Hope's arm and neck. *Keep walking,* she thought. *Do NOT look back. Why haven't we crashed yet? What was that? Juice?* Slinking back down into 23C, she plugged her ears with headphones and closed her eyes. Half an hour passed in a cocoon of humiliation, darkness and jazz.

When the pilot announced the final decent into Denver International Airport (DIA), he informed passengers that it would be abrupt. He did not lie. Ten minutes later, they were on the runway. He turned on the intercom once more and said, "The National Weather Service is calling this a blizzard, making flying treacherous. The airport has officially been shut down. When you deplane, please check in with one of our friendly ticket agents. They will help you reschedule flights when the weather lifts. Happy Holidays! We hope your stay in the Mile High City is a pleasant one."

Stranded in Denver? thought Hope, breathing easier now that she felt terra firma. She dabbed at the juice drops on her blouse with a paper towel. It occupied her until the other passengers deplaned. Ten minutes later, she emerged from the jetway, wondering how long she would be stranded.

A voice called her name. She spun around, surveying the terminal crowd. An orange juice-stained white shirt approached from her right, its wearer calling her name again. He wore a ball cap and tinted sunglasses and waved. *I know that face,* thought Hope. *OMG! George!*

Chapter 12

Hope's short list of things to do during an airport lockdown: sniff out the free wi-fi, weigh the benefits of proper hydration against the expense of $4 bottled water or, if poetically moved, record observations. There were no shortage of them now.

"If you would *rotate your tires*, I wouldn't be *stuck* in Denver!" a man seethed at an airline agent.

"Don't Happy Holidays me!" another bellowed, thumping his chest. "Show me, don't tell me. Give me some blow money or a duty-free pint. Do something. And stop smiling and apologizing."

Such raw emotion was rarely wasted on Hope, in times when had-a-bad-day greeting cards wrote themselves. Or would have written themselves, but for the stain before her.

At the sight of it, Hope's lips parted, but nothing came out. *I nearly plowed GEORGE over on the airplane!* she thought. Her throat thickened. "Come with me," she suddenly declared, or rather she heard the crisis-version of herself say. She motioned for him to follow. "We can't have you looking like that."

George tugged down his cap and matched her pace in silent compliance. *Guess I better stick with my handler,* he thought.

In the minutes that followed, Hope bought him a fresh orange juice and located a men's apparel store. She had him fitted in a new white, button-down collar shirt. After charging it to her credit card, she said, "I should have figured that after my flight was cancelled, I'd bump into you on the next one. Obviously, I underestimated the bumping. But look at you now. Good as new. On to the next crisis! I suppose we should check on our luggage."

"I can't risk being spotted in that mob," said George, looking back at the gate.

"Oh, right. I suppose not." Hope nodded like she understood all about being famous.

"You hungry?"

"I could eat." She followed George's gaze. "The Chophouse, huh? Barbecue. You sure you want to risk another white shirt around me?"

"Bring it," said George, leading the way. "I lived in a frat house once upon a time. I'm still at least half zoo gorilla."

"You hide it well."

"What I don't consume, I usually fling, but I suppose I can't risk being spotted doing that here either."

Hope snorted, then quickly clapped her hand over her mouth. *At least my lungs aren't collapsing,* she thought,... *yet. He's looking at me again, and now I'm going to have to chew and swallow.*

After being seated, they studied the menu. *Did he see me hovering too or just hear me scream?* wondered Hope. *Maybe I don't want to know. He's probably too much of a gentleman to bring it up. I've almost forgotten how to act around a gentleman.* She peeked over her menu. *Just be yourself, only different.*

"Something wrong?" asked George.

"Oh, um, no. What looks good?"

"I'm tempted to go with the salmon. Probably rolling the dice there. Although I suppose it wouldn't be too much trouble to fly it in fresh daily."

"A fine choice," confirmed the waiter, appearing with a carafe of water. He filled two glasses, lit the candle and read their faces. "It is a fresh, no-regrets salmon. Served on a bed of wild rice with grilled asparagus tips. The lemon beurre blanc sauce is like a kiss on the lips."

"Long, slow and rapturous, I hope," chuckled George. "Obligatory pecks are hardly worth mentioning."

The waiter nodded as though his mind had been read.

"It's settled then," said George. "Salmon for me and the house special for the lady."

Hope tilted her head, wondering how he knew that she wanted pork chops. Then she noticed her finger pointing at them on the menu.

"Oh! Pardon me," said George, leaning toward Hope. "I have neglected your starch."

"The white cheddar mashed potatoes, please."

"I would have guessed that."

Would have guessed that? thought Hope. *One look at me and he sees mashed potatoes? That's what happens, I guess, when you are used to dining with the bulimic. Paige probably would have ordered half a crouton. Why can't I be Paris thin?*

"Forgive the intrusion," said the waiter, his eyes narrowing at George. "But aren't you …."

"No. I just look like him," said George. "What do they call that again? Doppleganger. If I looked like Elvis, there might be some money in it." He pointed a finger to the weather radar on the far wall. "Now what can you tell me about that?"

The waiter huffed. "We're stuck here for a while. Some of us more than others. At least you don't have to work. Anyway, I just heard that the Department of Transportation shut down the interstate, so ..."

"Just like I planned it," George broke in, then turned to Hope again. "How about some wine?"

"Why not?" Three weeks ago, she had talked wine with the Unmatchables – etiquette and the importance of avoiding potent reds, champagnes, ice wines and ports on first dates. "No cheap wine, gentlemen," she had instructed. "And nothing bone dry or overly sweet. Order a bottle of something you imagine your date drinking with her lady friends. Or if you are uncertain, pick a conversation starter: Mad Housewife Cabernet, an Oops Chardonnay or a Conundrum red or white. When it is poured, sip. Don't chug. It's not beer. Wine is a tell, a show of your sophistication. It reveals that you are sensitive to your date's wants and are willing to fork out money on something other than golf."

At present, Hope listened with interest as George discussed Portuguese whites with the waiter – wines unknown to her. Their names enchanted – Fitapreta, Quinta da Pellada, Casal Figueira. Her eyes drifted to the flickering candle in the middle of the table. *What kind of tell is this?* she wondered. *How do I read this wine? There probably is no tell other than it is being ordered by a real gentleman, not one in the making. And a celebrity to boot. Millionaire wine. This is a first.*

"What do you make of that one?" asked George.

Hope looked up, surprised to find the waiter gone. "Sorry?"

"The candle. Looks like you are on the verge of christening again. I'd be lying if I said I weren't curious."

"I'm a bit gun shy after last time."

George slid the candle toward himself. "It falls on me, then," he said, sniffing. "I got nothing. Must be a dud."

"Probably unscented."

"You sure it's not a scratch and sniff?"

Hope giggled. "You're in a good mood for being stranded."

"What's not to like?" George panned the room. "The food is coming. Good drink is on the way. You got the Chop House vibe. And no meetings for days."

"And good company," added the waiter, reappearing. He presented the wine bottle, uncorked it and poured a sample. "Ignore me unless there's something I can do to make your dining experience more pleasant. It's been months since I've heard such a melodic tête-à-tête."

George swirled his glass, sniffed and sipped before nodding his approval.

"Good company," repeated George, raising his glass after the waiter filled it. "I'll drink to that. Better than good, actually. To the company then, and the way she mitigated the shirt crisis."

They clinked. Hope took two sips that bordered on gulps.

Holy! she thought. *Awesome wine! Better than good company? Me? Better not read into it. Although a couple more sips of this and I can probably handle another wink. Maybe. But absolutely no un-tucked feelings. Oh God! He's looking at me like that again! Coffee shop look take two.* "Apes!" she blurted.

"Apes?" George scrutinized his wine glass.

"April. A friend of mine. I forgot to text her when we landed. Sorry. This will just take a sec." *stranded n denver,* she typed on her cell phone. *sipping wine with the boss.*

George refilled their glasses to half full, "an optimist's glass" he called it. When the entrees arrived, conversation ebbed and flowed between favorite cuisine, most dreadful meetings survived and previous travel inconveniences. There were no awkward silences.

After dessert, a ginger coconut crème Brulee, they checked on their luggage. By then, angry passengers had dispersed. The ticketing agent informed them that they could not get their bags until morning. He distributed blankets, pillows and apologies, then picked up the microphone. "We regret to inform you that passengers will not be allowed to sleep on airplanes," he announced. "Please make yourselves comfortable in the terminal." He cut the mic and whispered to his counterpart.

"No, you idiot!" snapped his co-worker. "Adding that it's just like camping is not a nice touch. Stick to the script."

He cleared his throat and flicked on the mic again. "Have a pleasant evening, and thank you for flying United."

"Touching," said George. "I wonder what they pay these guys." He grabbed pillows and blankets and offered one of each to Hope.

She retreated a step. "Um, sorry."

"For?" George raised his eyebrow.

"Well, it's just. I need to go shopping."

"Okay. Where are we going?"

Hope shook her head. "I've burdened you enough for one day. I can manage this one alone. Besides, I wouldn't want you to risk being spotted again."

"Just checked my itinerary. Will you look at that? Nothing for days if the meteorologist is right. What else *is there* to do?" He lowered his cap. "Lead on, handler. Got your blankie and pillow right here." He tucked them under his arm and patted them.

"When do you suppose they last washed those blankets?" asked Hope as they browsed in the first store. "And the pillows. Ewww." She shuddered. "I'd need to see them under a microscope before surrendering my head to one. They're probably infested with bed bugs or dysentery. Just how many people touched those pillows?"

"Millions, no doubt," answered George. "What are we shopping for?"

"New blankets and pillows. Untainted ones."

At the second store, she found bedding. George examined the tag on her new blanket. "Someone in Peru touched this one. What's the dysentery situation like down there?" He chuckled and pulled out his wallet. "I got this. We're on business."

He then purchased bottled water, snacks, a book light, two sets of slippers and toothbrushes, toothpaste, a variety of magazines, a Scrabble board and anything else that captured Hope's eye for more than a few seconds. Text alerts chimed on her cell phone as the shopping bags accumulated. She ignored all but one from her father:

You have Mom worried, it read. *Please call.*

busy now, Hope typed back. *i m n good hands. call u n an hour or 2.*

Hope's mind was too occupied with the present for more texting. *Who is this man? – finding adventure in being stranded, toting shopping bags without complaint and showering me with a fresh supply of sanitizing wipes and both kinds of Cheetos. He's been firing those holy crap blues all evening, and I'm still mysteriously coherent. Must be the wine. Note to self: Add Portugal to the Bucket List.*

There was no luggage update when they returned to the ticketing counter. Hope and George found only one suitable prospect for sleep: a blue bench without armrests facing away from the windows. The double panes behind it blocked the snow and wind, but not the chill. The cold clung to the bench, it seemed, and was, in fact, the reason that it had been passed over by others. It would sleep only one, albeit not comfortably.

"I'll take the floor," said George. "Don't worry. I've got these infested airline blankets and pillows to cushion the blow."

Hope consented, provided that George join her on the bench (after she sanitized it) for bedtime reading "before the carpet claimed him." He affixed the book light to the back of the bench and joined her. Wrapped in blankets, they huddled close. The spill of light slanted between them as they flipped through magazines for the better part of an hour. Words were few, except when Hope, just before turning in, phoned her parents.

When George retired to the floor, he uttered a faint "hmmm."

"What is it?" asked Hope in a half whisper.

"A curiosity. I wonder how many Peruvians touched your blanket during the manufacturing process. Maybe it's automated. Then again, we're talking about Peru. What's the old saying? Many hands make light work. Oh well. Try not to lose any sleep over it."

"You know what else they say?"

George yawned. "Dare I ask?"

"Sometimes, it's the little things, like bacteria."

"Ah, the little things. First the candles, now the bacteria. What next?" He yawned again and said no more.

The sound of his unconscious breathing soon filled Hope's ears. *I can't say I saw this day coming,* she thought, recalling the morning bluebird and April's interpretation: joy, ecstasy, love. She curled up in her blanket and fluffed her pillow, entertaining George's words once more: "… how many Peruvians touched your blanket?" She rolled the tag between her fingers. *And YOU touched this, George Springs. How is it that your germs don't feel dirty at all?*

Grabbing her cell phone, she texted her mother before drifting off: *2day was sooo not a 4.*

Chapter 13

By morning, the storm had swelled and now stretched from the Rocky Mountains to the Midwest and curled north and east. And now it had a name: "The Day after Christmas Blizzard." Everyone, it seemed, knew someone whose holiday travel plans had been upended by it. In response, 24-hour news channels expanded their weather forecasts. The blizzard *was* the news.

From broadcast studios, news anchors fake-shivered, sympathizing with their field correspondents, who shouted live reports into microphones – coats flapping, voices straining, frostbite nipping at their extremities. "I have never seen such fine flag-pole-licking weather," one quipped.

The crown jewel of the blizzard story was the 3,000-plus travelers stranded at DIA. The TV networks clamored to gauge the misery index inside. What was going on in there? The viewing public wanted to know. "I'll tell you what it's like," said one stranded passenger who phoned in to *Today's Weather Channel.* "It's torture! My loafers are in my (bleep, bleep, bleep) suitcase. The airline won't release them. (More bleeping). Some crock about homeland security. I've had the shoes I'm wearing shined four times just for the massage. They give you that look here if you don't tip."

Another news station aired split-screen coverage, contrasting the present storm with DIA's previous holiday shutdown blizzard. "As you can see on the right, not as much falling snow as the blizzard of 2006," said the weatherman in a crescendo-ing voice, "or to be more accurate, not yet. In 2006, more than 20 inches of snow fell in a 24-hour period, and DIA was grounded for 45 hours, stranding thousands. However, *this* storm is packing a much bigger wallop. Snow accumulation should surpass 20 inches sometime tomorrow afternoon. Travelers could be stranded at the airport for the better part of a week."

The romantic frosting of the terminal window panes the night before had illuminated with the dawn into an ominous blur. There wasn't a single runway in sight. Nor a visible landmark on the horizon. Just a swirling white fury. Wind whistled and howled. Snow pinged the windows. The assault struck unconscious chords in the stranded, the way a fire in a hearth enchants, only with an added sense of helplessness. The only power strong enough to break its hold was the aroma of brewing coffee.

After a silent stare out the windows, Hope and George followed their noses. They fell into the nearest coffee line, surprised to find it animated. Overnight, it seemed, a transformation had swept through the terminal. Complete strangers now took interest in each other – Where are you from? When did you arrive? Did you sleep last night? They offered the use of their cell phones to those with dead batteries. The collective goodwill – absent in most just 24 hours before – was palpable, radiating outward, even spilling across the counter.

"Did you make this brownie yourself?" asked a whiskery, middle-aged man with circular-framed glasses. He licked his lips and smiled at the barista. She was half his age, had a pixie haircut and the complexion of a goddess.

"From scratch this morning," she answered.

"So this is where the magic happens, huh?" said the man. "Well, I guess I'll have to marry you then."

The barista flashed an engagement ring. "Take a number. My man, Alfonse, is in line ahead of you."

"Oh, didn't see that. Alfonse, huh? Well, I'm an attorney. I represent clients going through divorce. Here's my card." He offered her one. "Not that you'll ever need it. I mean, I hope you never need it, but in the unforeseen event that you are someday in need, I'm your man. For a negligible fee, of course. But maybe we can swap brownies for representation."

The barista pushed forward the tip jar. "Until then, maybe you can help me afford you."

"He's no match for her," said Hope.

"In more ways than one," agreed George, scrolling through text messages. "I better call Marbles. But that can wait. Clearly this brownie attorney needs us now. Oh, that reminds me! I'd like to get your two cents on the new ad. How about it – over coffee?"

Lines stretched across Hope's brow. She pulled up her cell phone calendar. "Checking my itinerary now: What do you know? Over coffee looks promising. I guess we'll have to leave Mr. Brownies-for-Representation to his own devices. He might survive. I'd say he's got a 50-50 chance of being match-able."

"You would know," said George. "Big of you to squeeze me in like this. I'm free until noon."

"What's at noon?"

"Lunch with you."

After getting coffee, Hope led George to the least filthy table. She wiped down the tabletop and chairs with sanitary wipes, then listened to George's trio of commercial spiels.

"Polished as usual," said Hope when he finished.

"That's it?"

"You were expecting?"

"More than that from you. Don't tell me what you think I want to hear. Everyone does that. Give me honest, candid, brilliant. The usual."

"Brilliant? On demand?"

"I read your reports."

Brilliant. Hope allowed the word to trickle inside, where others had long trampled. Except for April and her father, words like brilliant were never bestowed upon her. But the transparency in George's eyes and conviction in his tone rang sincere. *Brilliant! And he still reads my reports?* Doubt had crept in after seeing them accumulate in his inbox. She had no clue what he had been doing in his office since the accident, other than rumors of painting. "Okay," she said. "I'll bite. Here's my two cents: The camera loves you, but to be blunt, there's nothing different in Love by George ads than your competitors' – compatibility tests, relationship matches, soul mates. Same old, same old. Not unique. I bet potential clients tune out after five seconds. Nothing pops."

George eased back in his chair. "So make it pop."

"I dunno. A minor repackaging, perhaps? Something to freshen up your one out of five stat. Maybe a love lottery take."

"Keep going."

"Chances of winning the lottery: 1 in 18 million. Chances of a hole in one: 1 in 2,500. Chances of Love by George helping you find your soul mate: 1 in 5. What are you waiting for? Call now. Blah, blah, blah, fade to black."

George clapped. "See? Brilliant!"

Hope shrugged a shoulder. The love lottery pitch was a litmus test – the safest, not her best idea. It was a necessary precaution. Love by George was not her baby. Implying that it needed redressing at all was a risk, she knew. But now that George had bit, maybe it whet his appetite for more. "Although, technically, that's not unique either."

"So, what would unique sound like?"

"You would have to get a skosh more personal."

"I can handle a skosh." George swallowed the last of his coffee.

"Okay. What about this: Tell the world what love by George is – not the business, but what love means to you, personally?"

"Love? You mean the real deal?"

Hope nodded. "What is love according to Chicago's most eligible bachelor? It's a simple question. Answer that, and you've got an edge on your competitors."

"What edge?"

"You've got you," answered Hope. "The tabloids trip over each other chasing after you because the public is curious. All those potential new clients. Give them what they want: You paint. So paint them a picture of happily ever after."

At this, George pressed his lips together and flexed his jowls. He breathed through his nostrils and pierced Hope with a stare.

"Someone could script it for you, if you are worried about …."

"No need for that." George stood, grabbed the cups and retreated to the coffee line.

Couldn't just own brilliant and shut it, thought Hope, watching him walk off. *Had to push, didn't you?*

But the thought of getting personal was not new to George. His gut feel was that one such ad done right – the perfect 30 seconds of misty – could be worth the risk. *My definition of love,* mused George, picturing his next red carpet event. *How would people respond? Touching new commercial there, Georgie. Didn't know that you had feelings. Sounds like something Paige would say. She doesn't count. She's not people.* Still, he hesitated. But by the time he returned, thoughts of early retirement prevailed. "Let's do it," he announced.

"Really?" asked Hope. "Wow. I mean, really?"

George nodded.

"I've been whipping up an Oscar of an apology."

"For what? I asked. You answered. I've got a greeting card poet at my disposal. Not going to let that go to waste. Besides, we're just talking about love in general – a warm, fuzzy image, not a backstage pass to my personal life."

And so Hope grabbed a pen and her notebook. George began recounting the day he cashed out of Wall Street and started Love by George. While crafting his compatibility test, he frequented shopping malls, coffee shops and restaurants, taking notes about "real-deal couples" – an activity not foreign to Hope. She had invested as many hours if not more, she confessed, seeking inspiration for greeting cards.

"You too?" chuckled George. "What did you come up with?"

"Just poems. Easier to write than commercials."

"For you, maybe. Hit me with a few lines."

"Of forehead kissing, hand holding and cuddling? Before noon? You are an unusual man. Shouldn't we stay on task?"

"So I'm supposed to get personal, but you won't?"

"Oh fine." Hope flipped to the back of her notebook. Clearing her throat, she suppressed the passion in her voice.

> *"No alarms -*
> *clocks or sirens,*
> *that someday imagined;*
> *Just your touch –*
> *the feel of it!*
> *And the naked concern*
> *in your eyes;*
> *I am lost*
> *in the palpable contents,*
> *of a heart opened wide ...*

And, well, that's a few lines," she said, referencing her notes. "Your turn."

"Is there more?"

"That's enough canoodling for one morning, don't you think?"

"There's a word," said George. "Makes me hungry for Chinese. I'll have the canoodles for two please."

"Listen to you: Playing with words. We'll make a poet out of you yet."

"Think I have potential?"

"A certainty. Just keep playing. That's the key, I think, with words, and every little thing."

"Like candles."

"Words, uh, make phrases," stammered Hope. "Phrases make poems. I'm guessing yours will be – how did Ted put it? – less bust-out-the-Kleenex-like than mine."

"He said that? Ted had his own real deal for 30 years, you

know. Then Ellie passed. She was something. *They* were something. Not sure how anyone could ever be the same after that."

"Our Ted?"

George nodded.

"Seriously? I, uh …," said Hope, cocking her head. *And there it is*, she thought. *Passing judgment prematurely.* It was two parts ignorance, one part arrogance, she knew – the calling card of the naive, of gossipmongers, bullies and bigots. Nothing curdled her more than those quick to judge. Nothing, that is, except when confronted with the same inexplicable tendency within herself. She tried to imagine Ted as a loving husband and recalled the last words that she had heard him speak.

"You mean to tell me that you got a woman to hop a plane for you last weekend, Bob?" Ted had said during his last coffee run. "You dog! I can't even find one to wash my underwear."

That Ted? thought Hope now. "Hard to believe. We're getting sidetracked. Aren't we supposed to be discussing your real deal?"

"Well, I'm no expert, but I don't think it can be manufactured – frustrating, considering my line of work. The real deal either is or is not. The first sign of it, I think, is when someone takes a genuine interest in your day. Not small talk. Not the hellos and goodbyes and what's for dinners? *How is* your day? – someone asking and truly wanting to know. Why? Because meaningless time passed in his or her absence. Then, bang! It hits you. You realize that you're all in, and it wasn't a conscious choice." His eyes grew distant. "It's different from what most people experience: just trying to co-exist, always feeling alone whether or not you are with someone."

George glanced again at Hope. Her pen had stopped writing. "Last time I saw it, oh it's been a few years. There was a 70-year-old couple holding hands at a café, making golden anniversary plans. Still holding hands!" He shook his head. "There they sat, after all those years, still finding something more in each other.

You could hear it in the way they spoke. Watching them. Listening to them. It just spilled over onto you. You felt lucky to be around it. That's what we all want, I think – to be that couple – to be all wrapped up in the one person you already know everything about." He picked up his coffee cup and sipped. "You think there's a commercial in there?"

"Yes," mouthed Hope. She stood and dropped her pen. "Bathroom!" she announced, her throat catching. A single word thundered in her mind with the cadence of each step as she scurried away:

Crap!

Crap!

Crap ...!

Chapter 14

Hope did not have to "go." Her faux-emergency served a single purpose: to muddle the picture that George had painted. Holy-crap-grade, real-deal images occurred naturally in Hope's mind, independent of others' stirrings. They haunted her nocturnal thoughts, when solitude was her only companion. The dreams that followed were pure vanilla torment – a touchy-feely husband serving her egg-white omelets in bed, 2.5 self-cleaning children and a white picket fence corralling a non-shedding, poop-less dog that only barked at intruders. Someday dreams. Now this – George envying spouses who treasured each other for half a century. If another trip to the public restroom couldn't deliver a reality slap, nothing could.

She walked in on women jockeying for mirror space – blushing cheeks, penciling eyebrows and pulling hair into pony tails. Foundation bottles, eyeliners and lipsticks littered the counter. "You've *got* to try this, girls," said a 20-something brunette, passing a bottle of concealer. "It's life-changing."

By Hope's unofficial count, eight sets of hands fondled it. Then, every last one of them touched the counter. *This is worse than prom*, thought Hope, cringing. Brandishing a razor in one hand, one infester unzipped her jeans and mumbled something about hairy Italian women. She resembled April, with one notable difference: She had lost her neck to a tribal tattoo.

"I could *never* get a tattoo or a body piercing," Hope had once told April.

"And why not?" replied April, poised to defend the butterfly on her ankle.

"Well, for starters, the parlor table you sit on. When was it last sanitized? Who sat on that table? What assurance do we have that they weren't carriers of something? And what about the needles and tattoo supplies, all bunched together, touching each other, incubating things?"

April rolled her eyes. "You really think someone with the Bubonic Plague rode the table like a hobby horse?"

"That's exactly what I think."

Now Hope imagined the shaving Italian riding. Repulsed, she flipped open her phone and texted April. *ur look-alike is hogging the ladies room mirror.* After hitting send, thoughts of George's 70-year-old couple returned and the topic preceding it. *Why does he keep honing in on the little things? Is that just banter?*

Hope inhaled deeply. She had been smoke-free now for 97 days, 3 hours and 12 minutes. Her last cigarette was at the interview. According to her phone app, quitting had added 10.4 days to her life. And she had saved over $1,000. Her cravings had diminished, but hadn't permanently subsided. Struggling with one now, she shoved gum into her mouth and reminded herself not to chew like a cow.

u braved a public restroom? replied April. *sounds dire. u must really have 2 go. how's stranded life? got food? h2o? somewhere 2 sleep?*

i got a hard plastic bench, Hope typed back. *not 2 uncomfy. plenty of restaurants. thankfully, i don't have 2 brave the toilet right now. no complaints otherwise.*

no complaints? texted April. *who r u? what did u do with hope? shouldn't u b freaking over messed up itineraries & not having a proper bed, unless, oh! does this has something 2 do with george?*

if i have 2 b stranded, this works.

ahem! replied April. *what about george? what's it like being stuck in a mr. yum yum fairy tale. details!*

things r fine.

and??? don't make me use all caps.

and what?

GEORGE! replied April. *HELLO??? WHAT ABOUT GEORGE?*

what about him? he's drinking coffee – no cream, cane sugar. detailed enuf 4 u?

FINE! replied April. *will drag it out of u l8r. need 2 have an ends-justify-the-means chat when u return.*

about what?

c? i 2 can withhold info.

whatevs! typed Hope. *gotta go. george is texting. ta!*

She read his text: *The long-anticipated release of Flight 4441's luggage is suddenly upon us. Gate B22. Not far from your bathroom. Can you get in line?*

on it, texted Hope. She perfumed her wrists and neck and cringed one last time at the hairy Italian.

Several passengers beat her to Gate B22. More fell in line within a minute or two of her arrival. No familiar faces. Then again, she had blotted out their memory after screaming at skeleton man in the bathroom. Across the terminal, a Salvation

Army Santa with pale and drooping eyes stood ringing a bell. The sign at his side read "Volunteers needed. My relief is snowed in! You can make a difference. Please help."

Hope smiled with approval as her phone rang. "Hello?" she answered.

"Had to make a pit stop," said George. "Any movement there?"

"They just wheeled in the luggage carts. The ticket agent from last night appears to be coordinating the movement here. Could get interesting."

"Do I hear a bell?"

"Impressive," said Hope. "That's the sound of Santa taking donations. And looking for volunteers."

"Sign me up for an hour."

"*You*? Ha!"

George's voice lowered. "I'm serious."

"Serious serious?"

"Yes, I'm serious. I can't say it three times and keep a straight face. Although I can hide behind a beard, stand and ring a bell. So there's that. Besides, I've got an hour and change before my 12 o'clock. That's you. We have lunch plans."

We, thought Hope. *George and I. That we. Liking that we very much.* "Oh, that's right. *You're* my 12 o'clock."

"Nice. Before your memory fails you again, tell the big man relief is on the way."

Hope hung up and waved Santa over.

"Bless him," he said in a raspy voice, pleased at the news. "Someone always steps up. 'Tis the season for it."

His spirit caught Hope off guard. So did George's willingness to solicit the indifferent. "If only I had your faith in people," she said.

"There's more potential in people than this suit." He looked upon her the way that Mac did, like he was making an investment. "Looks like it's *your* time to step up." He pointed. Only one person now stood between her and the ticket agent.

George appeared moments later. After handing Hope his luggage ticket, he ambled off toward the donation kettle. Another text from April chimed.

stranded n the airport with nothing but time, it read, *& u have 2 bolt cuz of a george text … that's telling!*

"Someone broke into my suitcase!" bellowed the man in front of Hope. The lock dangled from his bag.

"I didn't break it," replied the ticket agent, curling his lip. "Your bag was inspected by the Transportation Security Administration. The airline is not liable for any damage."

"So theft in the name of Homeland Security, that's the gig?" piped the man. "You're selling my stuff on eBay, aren't you?"

"Bag inspections are standard procedure, sir." The agent offered a form. "Fill this out and return it. We sincerely regret the inconvenience."

"Yesterday, security confiscated my toenail scissor. Now this. Ever had an ingrown toenail? If my feet weren't ice cubes right now, I'd take off my shoe and show you a real threat."

"Next," said the ticket agent, waving Hope forward. "Luggage tickets?"

She presented them. He compared the tags to those on the luggage carts and returned with a frown. "Sorry. Not here."

"What do you mean not here?" asked Hope.

"No bags."

"I checked my carry-on when I boarded. So did my boss. How could our bags be gone? Did you lose the airplane? It couldn't possibly have flown away."

"These things happen. It's too early to know at this point if your bags are temporarily lost or irretrievably lost, but one thing I *can* tell you: Your bags are at the moment unaccounted for. Happens to two percent of all luggage. Anyway, we hope to know soon, one way or the other, the fate of your bags. Usually takes a week, sometimes a month. Sorry. It's a big airline. We appreciate your understanding."

"That's just it. I *don't* understand. How do you lose checked bags?"

He held out another form. "The airline will compensate you if they don't turn up. Not much from what I understand. But it's something. I'm truly sorry for your loss."

"Where did they find you?"

"Missouri."

"The Show-Me state?" muttered Hope. "Did they expel you? You can't even show me checked bags." The sight of George – the tightest-belted Santa she had ever seen – stopped her shaking head.

"No bags?" asked George.

"They're sorry for our loss." Hope tried repelling a grin. "Not used to seeing you like this."

"Remind me to bring my tailor next time. I need to pork up a bit to have some street cred." He yanked up his pants. "Better?"

"I've seen worse."

George opened his wallet and pulled out a credit card.

"What's that for?" asked Hope.

"No luggage, right? You need clothes."

"Maybe after lunch."

"Or before," said George, turning at the sound of jingling. "And Merry Christmas to you, sir!"

A passerby deposited coins into the kettle. "Where's your belly, Santa?"

"I'm sucking it in." George patted his abs and turned again to Hope. "We can eat later, meet back here in say ...."

Hope shook her head. "I'll be over there." She pointed to the vacant chairs in front of Gate B22. "I have a fierce no-ditching policy for those who call me brilliant. Your brainwashing being so complete and all, I can't risk a relapse. Plus yesterday, I kind of got used to you toting shopping bags."

And so for the next hour, George performed Santa duties while Hope busied herself in her notebook. *Is she working on the new ad?* he wondered between donations. *Or another canoodling poem?*

On three separate occasions, Hope rested her pen and glanced up at George. He tried to recall the last time he was on the receiving end of such a look: beaming with the chin jutted forward, as though an innocence were being entrusted to his care. When she broke eye contact, the allure lingered. The hour passed quickly.

They lunched on sandwiches. Between bites, George probed Hope with a fresh curiosity – this time regarding her aspirations. She answered briefly, paying lip service to her coffee-shop-ownership and writing dreams before redirected the conversation to his volunteering. While listening to George's reply, she jutted her chin anew, as though his words were another wave of sunshine that she intended to wholly absorb.

"When I crashed, just before blacking out, I had an epiphany," George answered. "Life isn't what I thought it was. I don't want to die full of *what ifs* and *if onlys.*"

"Playing Santa was a *what if* for you?"

"More of a *why not.* Volunteering helps me see things I never saw before."

"There you go sounding poetic again."

"Am I? I call it graduate-level people watching. Speaking of which, I noticed you writing in that notebook of yours again earlier. Your pen dispensed ink for the better part of an hour."

"Just tinkering with your 70-year-old couple. I want to get it right."

"You will," said George, turning toward the window, staring at the flustering snow. "Looking forward to hearing it. We won't be going anywhere anytime soon, which reminds me, we still need clothes."

So off they went, in search of concourse wear. "Give it to me straight," said George when he would try on something. "How does this look?" Hope repeatedly muted the thought *nothing looks bad on a body like that.*

Shopping small talk centered on childhood memories: George's earliest recollection was getting an MMR shot at age three. Convinced that he was being euthanized like his neighbor's dog, he fled down the hospital wing away from the nurse's needle, screaming, "No! Don't kill me! I'll be a good boy!" Hope's first memory, also at age three, was dancing on condiment packages that her mother had dropped on the kitchen tile. Hope squealed with delight as streams of ketchup and mustard shot onto the cabinetry. More childhood memories – equally amusing and frightening – followed. They continued through dinner, Chinese food this time, until George turned inward, contemplating his fortune cookie message: Your dearest wish will come true.

"Well?" prodded Hope. "*What is* your dearest wish?"

"It *was* to build the business, cash in, then disappear on my yacht."

"And now?"

"I'm not sure." George rested his chin in his hand and pondered his rocks – his most prized possessions. He felt a detachment from them now, not just because they were 1,000 miles away. His eyes drifted to that place beyond focus where one takes silent inventory of past regret. After a good ten seconds, he cleared his throat. "What about you?"

"Right now?"

George nodded.

"I dunno. A poetic reading would be nice. I'm a sucker for parsed words."

"Hmmm. Well, I guess that's out, unless you want to share another one of your poems. All I've got is airport magazine articles, snacks and a game of Scrabble."

"Scrabble!" chirped Hope. "I'm sooo in. I forgot all about the new board you bought. Shall we?"

In haste, they returned to their sleeping quarters. George led the game off with "repartee" – 18 points on a double-word square, plus a 50-point bonus for using all seven letters.

Whatever affliction he suffered from his fortune cookie message vanished after he tallied the points and announced them. His resulting mood peppered the air. And as the game progressed, between chit-chat, Hope and George, at different intervals, both sensed the moment at hand. An invisible something. It affected many of the stranded, especially those whose digital devices died. Free from deadline and obligation, the world – whatever it was before Denver – shrank until only the person in front of you remained. And in that stillness, things grew. A subtle tweak of the lip. An engagement in the eyes. A letting down of walls. And countless other non-verbals that cumulatively took hold – all fluid and poetic, silently forming lines to read in between. But even in that alternate universe, Scrabble is Scrabble. And wordsmiths like Hope played for blood. It took her the balance of the game to surpass George's score. After eking out victory, she phoned her parents.

Covering the mouthpiece, she waved George over. "That's *not* what happened," Hope's mother's voice boomed. "I worked late last night. Decided to phone your father to make sure that he wasn't starving. Reminded him about the plate of stuffed herb goat cheese chicken in the fridge – the same thing he inhaled three servings of the night before. A dozen ingredients. I chased all over town tracking them down. So what does he do? He gives it to the dog and makes himself a peanut butter sandwich."

"Breathe, honey," said Hope's father in the background. "It's just leftovers."

"Ouch, Mom!" said Hope, her ear next to George's.

"Oh there's more," continued her mother. "*Then,* he loads the dishwasher. *Your* father. *Loading* the dishwasher. I swear he's trying to finish me off to collect on the life insurance."

After hanging up, Hope explained. "Mom never lets anyone load the dishwasher. Funny. You would think that dad, of all people, would know better. Anyway, when someone else loads it, she empties the whole thing, reloads it and lectures about putting things in their proper slots."

"You should retrofit her dishwasher racks," said George, chuckling. "That would be funny."

"It would be," said Hope, turning serious. "Funny, but wrong."

"Oh." George, backed away and held up his palms. "Sorry. No offense."

"I don't know where that came from." Hope clasped George's hand. "Probably my mother. Sorry. I have said worse. I'm just trying not to."

When they turned in for the night, George was stuck in reverie – contrasting Hope with his social circle, those always grasping for more, usually money or power. *None of them* ever focused on becoming a better human being. Not one would ever think "funny, but wrong."

Chapter 15

Burrowing beneath pillows and blankets did little to muffle DIA's late-night intercom announcements and ventilation rumblings. In between the clamor, a few glorious moments prevailed, when songbirds warbled. Everyone attempting sleep wondered if they were they real or a recording, but not enough to investigate. Instead, they tossed and turned, slipping in and out of slumber. Hope and George managed four hours of sleep after Scrabbling. Had George's phone not rung as the first dull rays spread across the horizon the next morning, they may have managed more.

"What part of 'call me' *don't* you understand?" snarled the voice on the other end.

"Ted?" said George, rising, straining for a focal point though the windows.

"Better go with Plan B. Playing dumb doesn't suit you, Sunshine."

"I was going to call …."

"Going to!" Ted's outburst startled Hope awake. "That's about as comforting *as your last* going to."

"My what?"

"I'm *going to* New Mexico. Remember that one? Don't worry. I'll be fine."

"Okay, you're right," said George, yawning. "I should have called. Look: I'd rather have your mutt lick me awake than this. I got busy yesterday and …,"

"Hold on a second," interrupted Ted. Rustling noises followed. "What is it now, Mary? Yeah, yeah. You're welcome. It's just a greeting card, not a kidney. Look I'm on with George now, so ..." He spoke into the mouthpiece again. "Busy doing what? You're stranded."

"We lost time shopping yesterday afternoon, and I ..."

"Shopping! I figured something *like this* would happen! Where's Hope?"

"Right here. Well, technically over there, sleeping, like I was doing before your syrupy wake-up call."

"Put her on."

"No. One of us starting the day like this is enough. There's no reason to violate her morning too." Peeking out from under her blanket, Hope mouthed 'thank you.' "I'm going now, old man," said George. "Go ruin someone else's morning. Got another call. Bye." He checked the number on the display screen and lowered his tone. "*You!* And to what do I owe this pleasure?"

Paige? wondered Hope. A pang. She had not shared George with anyone for two days. Now he traipsed away all chatty. She stared out the window. Snow battered the terminal with vigor undiminished. Cloaked in her blanket, she glossed over until his return.

"I need coffee," he said. "Ready to go?"

Hope managed a smile. "Born ready."

In the coffee line, George thumbed through the cash in his money clip. "How about something to eat too? What sounds good?"

"I should have fruit, but I find myself leaning toward a donut."

"A spontaneous lean? Probably a stray arrow from Cupid's bow."

"How do you figure?"

"There." George pointed to a young couple across the concourse. Oblivious to their surroundings, their faces seemed drawn to each other – like a kiss was imminent. "See? There's an arrow that hit its mark. Note the lean. You were probably collateral damage."

Oh God! thought Hope. *It's a metaphor! Look at me! I'm the freaking Tower of Pisa!* Her weight was resting solely on the foot closest to George, her shoulder inches from his. She hadn't consciously been closing the gap. "I could, uh, do worse than a donut," she stammered, retreating a step.

"Don't stop now." George's lip curled, dimpling his cheek. "Would you mind leaning again for me? I've never matched people with pastries."

"Chocolate-glazed. Top shelf," said Hope.

"And they say that love at first sight is antiquated. Not here. No wonder you leaned. Definitely more donut than hole here. Unless my eye deceives me, that hole is smaller than the standard sixteen-twentieths-of-an-inch. Two of those, please," he told the cashier after ordering coffee, "and toss in two cups of fruit."

"You measure donut holes?" asked Hope.

"No, no. Just something I read." He handed Hope her breakfast.

"What else you got on donuts?" She took a bite as they made their way to a table.

He replied in a documentary tone. "The first donuts were hole-less. They were solid pastry until Hansen something or another, a New England ship passenger, poked through mommy's deep fat fried bread. Yes, it was Hansen himself who is credited with the donut hole, a resume filler no doubt. Oh, you've got something on your, uh ...." George set his breakfast down on a table and pointed to Hope's face.

She shrugged.

"Here. I'll just, um ...." He nodded again and extended two fingers, then wiped frosting from the corner of her mouth. Reading approval in her eyes, he gently brushed downward on her lips. On the final stroke, his touch triggered their parting. She felt her bottom lip adhere to his fingertips. Their eyes locked. Several heart-pounding seconds passed. Then, as though a silent alarm had tripped, he blinked rapidly and pulled away, slowly releasing her like wobbled Jell-O.

Hope stood lip first, leaning again.

"Oh!" said George in a patchy tone, his gaze on her lip. "Your OCD! How disgusting for you: My fingers. The germs. Sorry."

"No sorry!" said Hope, thinking, *Can we do that again?* Suddenly a fresh revelation struck. Her own fingers – three of them – were touching her lips, reliving the tingle. *Oh God no!* She jerked her hand away and sat down on it. Silence overtook her.

George had long regarded hiccups in conversation as allies. Few used them to better advantage than he did, to read beneath the skin. Only now, with this silence, he felt the urge to break it. "Well, there's no ignoring *that* now, is there?" he said, pointing to a scatter of crumbs on the table. It was the first meal that Hope had neglected to sanitize a surface that she had come into contact with. "I'll help you wipe."

"Right." Hope snapped out of her daze and placed two sanitizing wipes in his hand.

"So, about that new commercial, how is my 70-year-old couple coming along?"

"I've actually been working on something else, but …,"

"Let's hear it. You're already one for one this morning."

Hope stopped scrubbing.

"The donut, I mean," said George, taking a bite of his.

They sat. Hope flipped through her notebook and thought, *He'd wipe any woman's mouth, you uber-dork. He's a perfect, lip-wiping, out-of-your-league gentleman. He's only chatting you up because he doesn't have another phone call. Don't get sucked in.* "Who are we?" she began. "Not you and I, we. I mean we, the company. We are Love by George, right?"

George nodded and took another bite of donut.

"We peddle love but only offer dating services. That's glaring. Once there's a soul mate – poof! Bye, bye, client. Money out the door. But love – the real deal, full of ups and downs – should last a lifetime, right, at least in theory? Like your 70-year-old couple. What about them? What if they needed help?

Shouldn't they be on the radar too? Why not offer a full menu of love: marriage counseling, anniversary cruises, second honeymoon travel packages, Valentines events, the whole enchilada. Imagine Love by George helping people not only find, but also maintain, a lifetime of love. Love by George: no longer just a dating service, no longer just like your competitors. If that's not an opportunity for expansion, I don't know what is. I'm still working on the 70-year-old couple spot. It's not quite ready."

"That's good," said George. "Very good. Effective immediately: I'm doubling your salary. Oh!" he exclaimed, glancing down at his wrist. "Almost forgot. I've got an early Santa shift today." George hit speed dial on his cell phone and strode away. "I've got it this time, Ted!" his voice bubbled. "Well, technically, Hope got it. Great hire, that one ...." He threaded his way through the concourse crowd.

Hope sighed, thinking, *Soon, the blizzard will pass, and the curtain will drop on this fairy tale.* She stared at where George had sat – a cold, gray swivel chair. Unoccupied. It haunted and mocked and lumped her throat. As soon as the storm lifted, she knew, empty seats across from her would plague her mealtime future, just as they had in her past. She touched her lips again and felt invisible.

scrambled thoughts & turkey bacon, she posted on Facebook, instead of what she was really thinking: *he touched me.*

"Scrambled thoughts" prompted a couple of "likes" and one SPAM recipe from a high school classmate. Flustered, she phoned April. "What's the difference between banter and flirting? There ought to be a pee-in-the-cup test for that. Stupid frosting!"

"What are you talking about?"

"He touched me: my lips, his fingers. I think they lingered. How many seconds need to pass before a touch becomes a linger?"

April heard desperation. "Stop thinking." She broke into a thoughtful discourse about living in the moment and letting life come to you. Only one phrase stuck with Hope: "What have you got to lose?"

What indeed! thought Hope after hanging up. *What's the worst-case scenario here? I fling myself at George and then ...? I guess it could cost me my job.* But never before had the upside of risk looked so appealing. *Your unconscious is screaming here, girl! For once, listen!*

Chapter 16

A screaming id was a decade-old conundrum for Hope, something she first contended with in college. She ridiculed it back then, thinking it settled science. *My psyche prof sure takes his id seriously,* she had thought the day that he drew Maslow's Human Needs Triangle on the board and justified it with Freudian rationale. *Too seriously. If the world acted entirely on impulse, it would be in much worse shape than it is.*

Now she was older, introspecting in grays. A decade of suppressing her wants yielded mostly regret. Silently, she warred within. Especially right now. Smack in the middle of DIA, her id came calling. Fright gripped every fiber of her being. Yet she felt oddly intoxicated, like going over Niagara Falls in a barrel minus the fear of perishing on the rocks below. She was cornered. It happened the instant George touched her lips. Which set of regrets could she live with more – letting it go and wondering *what if* the rest of her life, or pursuing it, risking her dignity yet again? Feeling a desperate tug, she granted her id temporary Facebook status update powers (which she reasoned could later be dismissed as poetic nuance if things backfired): *All in again and if-ing up a storm,* she posted. *Time to run down that hill. Time to know.*

Yesssss! commented Danya, Hope's greeting card illustrator. *Found someone to make you smile?*

??New love?? another inquired.

April chimed in with comment number 12: *Woot! Keep us posted if you dare.*

A fresh commotion prevented Hope from reply. Coffee drinkers now flocked around the TV. "With more than three feet of fresh powder, digging out should take a day or two," the weatherman announced. "But here's the good news: Flights at DIA should resume sooner rather than later. Those stranded might return home by New Year's Eve or New Year's Day."

What!?! thought Hope. Lifting? Now? Must ... find ... George! After powdering my nose. And touching up my lips. I definitely need more touching. Touch me again, George. This time I will lean right into you.

George's hour had passed by the time Hope arrived. He conversed with the regular Santa by the donation kettle. "Me time," she interjected, sidling up from behind. Slinging her arm in George's, she tugged him away. "Don't worry, Santa. I've been on the nice list since, like forever."

"Later, Jimbo," George called back over his shoulder, struggling to keep pace.

"Jimbo?" repeated Hope. "Way to blow his cover."

"What's the crisis this time?"

"I need to know something." Hope reached with her free hand and slid it up George's bicep. *This id business is totally the way to go*, she thought, pulling in closer.

"Need to know what?"

"That *is* the question, now isn't it? You sir, are on a need-to-know basis."

"On a need-to-know about your need to know?"

"Exactly! Now where was that... bingo!" Hope yanked him into a trinket shop, stopping in front of the mood ring display. She slipped a ring on her finger and insisted that he do the same. Then, before he could object, she purchased the matching set.

"It's red," said George, contemplating the color. "If that doesn't mean hungry, we should demand a refund."

Hope grabbed his hand. "More of an imperial red or a lust ...." *Radiant palm*, her inside voice noted. *Un-chewed fingernails. Proportioned digits. Soft, yet firm to the touch. Like they were when they touched my lips.* She ran her thumb over his index and middle finger and cleared her throat. "… or orange-red if you prefer Crayola-speak."

"Lust?" George pulled away. "Well that's just, awkward. That was your need to know? You're right: I didn't need to know that. In other news, my donut just expired. How about this place?" He yanked Hope into the nearest restaurant, *Vino Volo.* After they were seated and ordered wine, he shook his head and mumbled, "Lust?"

Hope slid the interpretation chart across the table. "This would give my Unmatchables something to discuss on dates." It read:

> red – aggressive
> orange – daring
> yellow – content
> green – relaxed
> blue – pleased or subdued
> purple – conflicted
> pink – unhappy
> brown - restless

"No lust," said George, "just plain red. I don't see these interpretations inspiring anything. I need something more tangible. Tired and hungry, for instance, the cornerstones of every masculine mood. Hungry leads to tired. Tired leads to crabby or possibly vegetative or …,"

"Agreed," said Hope. "The chart is lame."

"I could have told you that before you had me fitted."

"Unless we tweak the interpretations. Make red hungry, or plead the fifth or one glass of wine away from flinging myself at you." She lifted her flute, swirled, then sipped, forcing herself to maintain eye contact beyond what felt natural. "Or something like that."

"So that's what the crisis was about, colors? To see if I was a true lust?"

"Think of it as market research for the Unmatchables."

Mood ring dates, mused George, the business angle surprising him. It provided another contrast from his social engagements, those Botox-revealing, ugly-whisperer gatherings. Hope percolated on, explaining how quartz shells and thermotropic liquid crystals reacted with body heat to produce color variation. As she spoke, it struck George that something as simple as color – more times than not – escaped his world of split-second black and whites.

"Well?" said Hope. "You in?"

George raised his glass. "Oh, I wouldn't miss this for the world. I'm *definitely* in."

Ravenous became the new red, they concurred. It conjured images of savagery. No telling what the Unmatchables would do with it, but it provided options to break silences or awkward non-silences. Options were good. "Ravenous," proclaimed Hope, extending her hand until George offered his. She slid her fingers underneath, resting her hand on the table, taking in the color of his ring again. "You must be full now. You're not ravenous anymore. You're bluish."

Bowls of chickpea chili arrived. They hashed out bluish and the remaining hues between spoonfuls. A color interpretation chart that "didn't suck" emerged. They agreed to monitor themselves for the next couple of days, taking note of when their rings changed colors, tweaking the chart as needed. *Your brilliant is showing again, girl,* thought Hope. *His hand is now yours for at least two more days.*

Though savoring the development, Hope felt like time – that finite mist – was doubling its pace. When daylight waned, she progressed from asking for George's hand to grabbing it without consent. His blueness eventually turned brown – smoky topaz according to Hope, "smarmy" according to the new chart. Purple followed, making its first appearance on Hope's ring as they traversed the concourse one last time before turning in. She thrust it into George's chest until he held her hand and studied it.

"Purple!" he proclaimed. He extracted the color key from his back pocket and unfolded it. "According to our chart, you are wildly conflicted."

"Wildly conflicted! Me? Never! That's a faulty interpretation. What do you say I am?"

"You have that same look in your eye now that you do after disinfecting. There's a word for that. It escapes me now. Something more eloquent than Dirtwad."

"Dirtwad!" repeated Hope, her lips spreading into a smile. Chin elevated, she exposed her neck fully, yielding it again after George had written off the gesture as a diurnal behavior.

He cocked his head.

"Dirtwad!" she mouthed as they resumed their stroll. *His subconscious just pet named me.* Reciprocating would be a risk, she knew, despite having gained free access to his hand. When she looked upon him at length, Mr. Yum Yum – April's nickname for him – was the only thing that came to mind. She couldn't call him that, though her id pressed.

Shortly thereafter, they settled in for the night, wrapping in blankets. Again, George positioned the book light between them on the bench. He perused a magazine. Hope attempted to match his industry, but failed. Barely a foot away, George sat slowly licking his fingers and flipping pages. *Would it kill you to lean just a little?* thought Hope. *To invade the shrinking space between us?* She bit the corner of her mouth and released a barely audible "mmm." Either George didn't detect it, or he pretended not to hear.

Hope gulped. *Here goes nothing.* Shutting her eyes, she dropped her chin and slowly toppled sideways. *You are sooo going to look like a loser if he pulls away. Leaning, leaning, leaning. Where is ....* Then it happened. Contact – a rush of warmth, strong cologne, a firm deltoid pressing back. Goose bumps radiated from her neck to her extremities. *Whatever you do, do NOT open your eyes. You ARE asleep. Sell it. Inhale.*

Exhale. Repeat.

Seconds ticked by in deafening silence. He made no movement and no sound, except that of soft respiration and the occasional turning of a magazine page. Time slowed again. By Hope's estimation, at least half of an hour passed without change. Finally, George clicked off the light.

His momentary shift allowed Hope to migrate. She nestled between his chest and shoulder. *Well, this REALLY doesn't suck!* she thought. *Probably just a sympathy shoulder, but I'll take it.* Her breathing eased to a rhythm rarely achieved, those nights – a few times a year – when there was no alarm clock, when dreams were too revealing to share, and sleep stole her away completely.

Just before losing consciousness, she felt George's cheek rest on her head.

Chapter 17

The drone of diesel engines. Hope stirred at the sound, increasingly aware of cold, hard bench pressing against her face. She sat up, clinging to her blanket. A purplish-tangerine hue splayed across the horizon, breaking the heavens with a promise – for those eager to depart. Overnight, clouds had dispersed. The wind had surrendered its fury. Snowplows treaded through a wall of snow, exposing tarmac in their wake. Hope's eyes watered.

"Just a sec," said George, his voice near. He lowered his phone. "Everything okay?"

"Too early for an assessment. Give me a minute." As Hope's eyes adjusted to the light, the past 24 hours looped in her mind. How long had it been since she felt this way? – since the present could not be improved upon. So long ago she couldn't remember. Maybe never. And now it was slipping away.

"Just reschedule it," said George, speaking into the phone again, "the sooner, the better. And get two tickets on the first flight back to O'Hare. I don't care what it costs."

Hope's eyes fell to George's bedding. It appeared disheveled, not neatly folded as it was the night before. *He didn't stay with me? Did I just dream that up?* Empty chest. It was a worse feeling than empty chair across from her at mealtime. She shed her blanket and skirted past George to the coffee shop.

"Hope?" he called out.

"Be right back."

"Oh, one more thing," he resumed, his voice fading. "Tell Paige I got her message and …."

"Can't neglect Paige now," huffed Hope, "can we?" *Oh to be a bulimic hottie!* she thought. *Another bang-up job of duping yourself there, Dirtwad. There's one for you: How NOT to Dupe Yourself. Step one: Lose the heart. It serves no useful purpose.*

Not duping yourself had yet to appear on the "How to" newspaper section that Hope read daily. The topic seemed no less practical than others, like *How to Look Taller* for instance, a compelling piece for 5-foot-nothings. Or *How to Flirt Your Way Out of a Speeding Ticket*. Surfing the web on her phone, she checked today's offering: *How to French Kiss*. "Perfect!" she muttered, skimming the pictorial of everything she would never do with George – snowflake kisses, breathing techniques and finding the tongue's sweet spot. When she looked up, the barista that had foiled Mr. Brownies-for-Representation was distributing samples.

"Happy New Year's Eve!" she said, presenting a tray of wee little cups. "It's called 'Joy' – our newest blend of tea."

"Perfect timing," said Hope. "I could definitely use a shot of joy." She picked up a cup, saturated her taste buds and swallowed. "Didn't take. You must've slipped me a cup of Jaded."

"Results vary. There's no betterment-of-spirits guarantee on the labeling. Just some gibberish about darjeelings and oolongs."

"Betterment. Good word. There's a tea name waiting to happen."

The barista shrugged, "How's your morning, hon?"

"In theory it could be worse."

"Glad it isn't worse." Smiling, the barista wandered off to circulate.

Look at her, thought Hope, *stranded at the airport, forced to work, serving up glad-it-isn't-worse right in the middle of my pity party.* Disasters, natural or otherwise, had no effect on someone like her, Hope sensed – one of those anomalies in life who could list things she was grateful for on her Facebook page every day for a year and end up with something more meaningful than clothes dryer lint traps. Hope stepped into line and reviewed *How to French Kiss* until it was time to order.

"What happened to you?" asked the cashier, stooping forward when Hope stood before her.

"'Scuse me?" asked Hope. "Is this about the Joy?"

"No. It's about your cheek. What *IS* that? Looks like a dime with holes." The cashier produced a makeup case from her purse and flipped it open.

Me touch that? thought Hope. She grabbed the cashier by the wrist and angled the mirror. The circular defect on her face was pinkest around the circumference, positioned halfway between her cheek bone and ear. "What the …?" *A nervous blotch? No. Too perfectly round for that. It's not a zit. Something I contracted in the ladies room?* She shuddered. *What IS that? It seems to be fading.* Then it hit her: *A perfect circle. Tiny hole impressions in the middle. A button! George's shirt! He stayed with me all night!*

"Oh my gosh! I love you!" exclaimed Hope, releasing the cashier's wrist. She held out her phone at arm's length and snapped a photo as her mood ring turned a vivid orange. *What's orange again? Who cares? New interpretation: Joy.*

She returned to her sleeping quarters clutching two steamy cups. Pressing George's coffee to his chest, she offered her chin anew. "For you."

"You sure perked up. I thought I saw tears."

"Huh?" Hope canvassed his shirt for evidence of her cheek. "Oh that. Happy leak. No worries."

George, followed her gaze down his shirt. "You leak, and apparently I dribble. Don't tell me we need to go shirt shopping again."

"Good to see the snow plows," she replied, then thought, *No it's not. Why did I say that?*

"Shouldn't be long now. Can't wait to get out of here."

Did last night mean nothing? wondered Hope, leaking anew, concealing it better this time. How could she ask for his shirt button now? A second ago, it was all she could do to keep herself from ripping it off his chest. Now this cold shower. *Is this the a-ha moment?* She recalled telling the Unmatchables what to do when it struck. *Withdraw immediately. Act as though NOT pursuing a relationship in your best interest. Be glad you didn't waste more of your time chasing down a future that won't happen. And absolutely no tears! At least until you are alone. Then let it go.* But there was no letting go of this. She spent the next several hours mentally recording the contours of his face.

When George caught her stare – over coffee, over lunch, on the in-betweens – he questioned it, simply asking "What?"

"What what?" replied Hope, once adding, "One of the six essential questions: who, what, when, where, how and why. Generally speaking, whys are more interesting than whats and lead to more interesting whys." Intended to sound playful, it came out flat. George's eyes absorbed her darkening mood. In them, she was lost and simultaneously found.

He did not press. Instead, he did what she could not: He moved on, monitoring weather reports in detail. By early afternoon, DIA announced that flights would resume the next morning. He phoned Madeline and scheduled meetings so that he could "hit the ground running."

You go, George, thought Hope. *Hop that return flight to reality. At least one of us still can.* Late into the afternoon, she checked her online horoscope:

Today is a crossroads: a five or a ten. It depends entirely upon you. In one direction lies the familiar, a security blanket of predictable but temporary comfort; in the other, the unknown, page one of an unwritten diary. Either way, the path ahead is clouded. What will you do? Think second, act first.

It was too late for that. Her id was already back in its box. Had George not intervened later that night, a horoscope five would have been inevitable. "It's almost the New Year," he said, grabbing her hand. "You need to smile again. C'mon."

He led her to the New Belgium Hub, a stuffy but tidy bar

and grill. Streamers crisscrossed beneath heating ducts. Suspended balloons swayed in between. A jazzy rendition of *"What Are You Doing New Year's Eve"* filled the space below. Patrons indulged in microbrews, well-plated appetizers and each other's company. Hope and George found barstools in front of a window, adjacent to a wall adorned with a red cruiser bicycle. While George contemplated the beer on tap, Hope sat, elbows on the table, resting her chin, and monitored the snowplows beneath the starry sky. *I definitely need wine tonight, not beer,* she thought.

At 10 o'clock Mountain time, the ball dropped in Times Square. All eyes drifted to the TV monitors. The coverage then shifted to Chicago for an hour's worth of man-on-the-street interviews and musical performances. At the top of the next hour, 11 o'clock Mountain time, fireworks exploded over Lake Michigan's Navy Pier, illuminating the 15-story Ferris wheel. Nothing worth saying came to Hope. In silence, she stole glances of George and sipped pinot grigio. *There is no other man in the world you would rather be with tonight,* she introspected. *So why are you such a drip? Why is it impossible to enjoy the last day of anything good?*

The crowd swelled to standing room only as midnight approached. The barkeeper, all eyebrows and sideburns, dimmed the lights and pushed up his arm garter. "Let's make a memory," he shouted. "Like right here, right now, in the kinship of your fellow blizzard mates. It's New Year's Eve, people! We all just survived another rat lap around the sun! Time to celebrate! Your next drink is on the house if your toast is worthy. Simple as that. Where you are from? What are you drinking to tonight?"

Patrons hoisted their pints.

"To the next airplane," the first responder, a Canadian, shouted. The crowd cheered in approval. "That overdue, much-ballyhooed flight home. Off with you all now, to your collective hopes and dreams. May they be delayed no more."

Others chimed in from Yonkers, from Murfreesboro, from

Pea Ridge and Cooter, from Hellhole Palms and as far away as Nobber, Ireland. They toasted friends, family and the one that got away. They toasted the bartender's generosity, the end of the blizzard and the year to come. Just before midnight, the toasting ran its course, and the crowd turned inward, searching for those who had not yet toasted. That's when George was identified.

"Come on, Georgie-boy," the spotter shouted. "Can't we get no love?"

George stood and removed his cap, which he had worn every day to conceal his face. He raked his fingers through his hair, then hoisted his pint to ohhhs and ahhhs and flashing cell-phone cameras. "Sure, I'll play along. I second Canada's hopes and dreams and add to them second chances, and microbrews on the tap, and passing the evening so agreeably."

"Who's the chick?" shouted the spotter.

Such is the litmus test of celebrity: What to do when publicly pressed after taking every precaution to remain hidden in plain sight? One ungracious reply and the adoring public forever turns on you. This played in George's mind as he raised a hand. The crowd quieted. "That *chick* ...," he said, pausing, "is my, um, poetry tutor." He glanced at Hope and bulged his eyes. "Why, just today I scratched down a few words and thought that maybe, perhaps, as uphill as the task may be, that she's infusing some of her talent into me."

"Let's hear it!" the spotter retorted.

"Well, I ...," stammered George.

A "Geor-gie!" chant ensued, mushrooming until he raised his hand again. "Well, I suppose." He removed a folded napkin from his pocket and held it up. *Showmanship 101*, thought Hope. *Good way to lure potential clients*. A hush fell over the room as he slowly unfolded it. "Most people don't share your enthusiasm for poetry. Then again, as you may know, *I am* in the industry of love."

The crowd cheered.

"Mind you, I'm new at this, and this is just a first draft. On second thought, I'm not sure it's ready."

"Read it! Read it!" roared the crowd.

"As you wish." He cleared his throat. "Here goes nothing: THOSE eyes of yours …."

Is he making this up on the fly? wondered Hope. *He couldn't have written a poem today. I would have noticed that, wouldn't I?*

"And *that* smile," continued George, glancing again at Hope, for reassurance she thought. She nodded back, rapt in curiosity. He let several seconds pass before resuming with a crackle. "And that heart, that wonderful, didn't-see-it-coming, knock-me-on-my-butt-while-stranded-in-DIA heart. *Your heart* …."

Now, the audience clapped. Then George turned toward Hope. In sobering baritone, he read on. "That heart. *Your heart* filled with all things worth exploring …."

The crowd awww-ed.

OMG! That's not the alcohol talking, thought Hope. *He's only had one beer.* She rose from her chair and touched her chest. Her eyes sparkled with invitation.

"Almost done," said George, scanning the crowd once last time. Hope could hear her heart pounding in her eardrums. "Let's see. Where were we, Dirtwad? The eyes, the smile, and ah yes, the heart. *Your* heart." He cleared his throat again. "So long have I waited to see just this …."

Midnight struck. The New Year! It would have been forgotten had not the barkeeper killed the lights and shouted it. *Auld Lang Syne* played. Confetti fell. The crowd embraced and toasted and fired off noisemakers.

Setting down her wine glass, Hope took one step forward. George leaned down and whispered the final words into her ear: "in anyone."

Hope's last step was a plunge. With both hands, she pulled his head downward until every patch of skin beneath her nose to the bottom of her chin pressed against his. She felt his hands cradle the small of her back. He exhaled slowly between kisses.

The sensation nearly collapsed her. Warmth cascaded through her in waves. It was an all-in kiss. There was no awkwardness. No question marks. No doubt.

The moment her lips touched his, she knew.

Chapter 18

"Hope, Hope?" A voice spoke into her dream.

The kiss! "Mmm," she moaned, "again." She turned over on the terminal bench. Once more the voice intruded. She opened her eyes, straining into the fluorescent light. The silhouette of George's face came into view.

"Your plane ticket," he said, fully dressed, down on one knee, placing it in her hand. "I couldn't get us both on the same plane. My flight is boarding now. Yours departs in four hours. Get some more sleep. See you back in Chicago."

"Mmm-kay," said Hope, her eyelids closing again. "Wait. Whaaa...?"

He was gone. No hug. No kiss. No nothing. Hope bolted upright. Her mind caromed back and forth, but mostly back to the night before, when her heart had skipped ahead. Her mood ring grayed. *See you back in Chicago? When? What kind of seeing? Like last night seeing? Or employer-employee seeing?*

Meaningless coffee followed – coffee for one, fruit, no donut, nothing poetic. *How did I do this before?* she wondered. A cold farewell was all that remained, a parting that erased the certainty of last night. See you in Chicago. Like Denver never even happened.

Not even her first-class seat pierced the numbness she felt. Not until she picked up a newspaper. That's when she saw the headline: NEW YEAR'S KISS BY GEORGE. Subtitle: Who's that Girl? The accompanying photo was blurred, a cell phone shot by the look of it. It exposed George's profile, confetti raining down, his lips locked with hers. Only Hope's chin shone prominently. The rest of her body tapered out of focus. The story read:

(Denver, Colo.) The midnight kiss: a New Year's tradition. Stranded at DIA by The Day after Christmas Blizzard, world-renowned matchmaker George Springs puckered up and planted one last night at straight up 12 o'clock. But whom did he kiss? Eyewitnesses at the New Belgium Hub were unable to positively identify the brunette that Mr. Compatibility simply referred to as his "poetry tutor." Has the country's most eligible bachelor finally met his match?

OH! MY! GOSH! thought Hope.

The article continued, touching on the Love by George Compatibility Test, George's stock market beginnings and how he had been spotted at numerous venues with Paige Walker, a *Chi-Town Trib* reporter. "There is no known engagement to her," the article stated. *Good to know,* thought Hope. One source recounted George's poem. "Something about her eyes and heart," the eyewitness said, "and getting knocked on his butt. I was ready to kiss him myself when he read it." The story concluded with: "The poem's last line, which George whispered into his tutor's ear just before kissing her, remains a mystery."

Hope embraced the paper and inhaled deeply. Today's fresh ink was last night's cologne. *That was NO kiss goodbye.* She pored over the article again, oblivious to the 747's takeoff. Nearly two and a half hours later, she scarcely felt the landing.

The flight attendant spoke over the intercom: "Flight 2998 passengers, welcome to O'Hare International Airport and the Windy City of Chicago, where it is currently 42 degrees and overcast. You'll need an umbrella out there today. There's rain is in the forecast. Local time is 2 PM."

Hope checked her voicemail. Two messages: one from her mother, one from April. Nothing from George. *Well, he HAS been gone a week,* she reminded herself. *He's probably being pulled in 100 different directions right now.*

After the drive home, Hope steeped a cup of mint tea. She booted her laptop and skimmed through emails and Facebook posts, ignoring two Scrabble requests, though longing for a second cup of repartee. *I wonder if George Scrabbles online.* She clicked on the TV for noise. *We could Scrabble like bunnies.*

"A New Year's Eve to remember," a voice blared. The *Mile-Hi Post* photo of George kissing Hope flashed on her TV monitor. Hope's face was blacked out, covered with a white question mark. "Online dating's most eligible bachelor puckers up," the narrator continued. "But who's that girl? How long did they kiss? All the juicy details on the weekend edition of Entertainment Buzz, starting right now."

Hope fell to the living room couch, paralyzed.

The host teased the story until the program's end, 25 minutes later. "Entertainment Buzz confirms that last night, online matchmaker George Springs III – stranded by the Day after Christmas Blizzard – rang in the New Year at a Denver International Airport pub. Take a look at this." The newspaper photo re-appeared, this time revealing Hope's face and chin. "Mr. Compatibility showered his affections on a yet-to-be-identified high-heeled brunette. Sources confirm that the couple kissed for half an hour before disappearing down the concourse together in festive spirits."

Every electronic device in Hope's possession began chiming – her phone, her notebook, her laptop.

Watching "The Buzz," a Facebook comment from a distant cousin read. *I know that chin. Fess up!!! You and George Springs? I want your life.*

Karli, the Love by George receptionist, texted: *Kiss and tell! Kiss and tell! If this is what "if-ing up a storm" produces, sign me up.*

The *Mile-Hi Post* photo suddenly appeared on Hope's computer monitor.

And to think I knew her when ..., a college classmate

commented, posting and sharing the image on her Facebook news feed. *Waaay jealous!*

The answering machine sprang to life next, broadcasting a stream of voicemail messages. She filtered them out, still glued to the kiss on TV. The image brought back the taste of his lips – all soft and pillow-y, much more of a hello than a goodbye taste, despite the abruptness of his parting. How could she not trust that kiss? Especially now after seeing it on TV.

C*N*N picked up the story next – the same who's-that-girl teaser, only taking a Cinderella slant: "… the last line of the poem, it seems, is still missing – not unlike a fairy tale glass slipper," said a reporter. "We now have confirmation that the lucky girl is from the Chicago area."

*Is C*N*N Facebook stalking me?* wondered Hope. Somehow, it had pieced together most of the poem. "But what did George whisper?" the reporter continued, on location inside the New Belgium Hub. "It remains the question of the hour, on the day after."

Hope checked her phone again. Her mother had left a voicemail: "Last to know again!" she griped. "Apparently, the whole world comes before me. Will Hope call, or will her mother continue making up stories for the neighbors? Inquiring minds want to know."

Her father then texted: *Found our dear Hope today. On TV! Mother is already naming grandchildren.*

Hope flipped to F*O*X News. It too had added the story to its rotation, deferring to a shrink for analysis. "What effect does making national news have on an ordinary person, someone like George Springs' new love interest?" asked the anchor.

"Probably similar to someone experiencing Sudden Wealth Syndrome, like say a lottery winner," answered the psychologist, Dr. Rissa, whose dark eyes danced over reading glasses. "Your life becomes a consumable. The masses suddenly know your face. Friends and relatives come out of the woodwork. Everyone wants something – a picture, an autograph, a piece of you. The attention can overwhelm – leading to anxiety, panic attacks, sleeping disorders, paranoia, depression, even guilt."

"Guilt? With all due respect, have you *seen* George Springs?" replied the anchor, rolling her tongue inside her cheek. "I'm pretty sure that one night with him would compensate for any un-pleasantry. Given the little we know of our mystery tutor so far – a poet, a right-side-of-the-brain type – are you able to draw any conclusions about her personality?"

"Well, I have a saying," answered Dr. Rissa. "According to psychologists, there are four kinds of people in the world, and I am not one of them. So I guess that's a resounding no. *Everyone* is unique, like any poet worth reading."

"What have studies revealed about the effects of sudden celebrity?"

"Recent studies show that more study is needed."

"Well, there's a surprise," chortled the anchor. "I'll ask it another way: You have studied human behavior for several decades. You heard the poem. What do you think he whispered?"

The camera cut away to the New Year's kiss before zooming in for the doctor's reply. "Studying and predicting are two different animals. If I could connect those dots.... Whatever he said, it inspired an agreeable response."

"Most agreeable," the anchor affirmed.

This can't be happening, thought Hope. *Me a national curiosity?* She wandered back to the answering machine in time to hear, "I thought you might need to talk, unless, of course, you have company. Company has been good lately, no?"

"Apes," said Hope, picking up. "What's up?"

"Oh it's all about you tonight, babe. Three hundred comments on your Facebook page, and counting. I was going to give you space, but ...,"

"I had no idea this would happen."

"Anonymity is overrated, except when it comes to your dreams. But hey, who needs dreams when you have *your* reality?"

Hope poked a finger through the living room blinds. "That's weird."

"What?"

"An SUV outside. I've never seen it before." Hope strained to distinguish the driver's features. He reached for something then glanced up. She pulled away before venturing another peek.

"Everything okay?" asked April.

"Fine. Looks like my neighbor got a new car. That's funny. He said he wanted a ... Oh God!"

"What?"

"A camera! He's a *freaking* paparazzi!"

"Do you want me to come over?"

Hope took a swallow of her now tepid tea. "No. I'm fine. I'll call you later. Bye."

She Googled *How to Duck Pappis* online and found:

1. Wear a disguise in public.
2. Be sneaky/no attention-grabbing behaviors.
3. If cornered, be cordial, not hostile.
4. Consider posing for photos instead of avoiding them.
5. Give up the limelight if you don't like it.

Duh! thought Hope. *I wasn't looking for the idiots guide.* Flustered, she resumed her channel surfing. The night passed without any new development. After midnight, she nodded off on the couch.

When she awakened the next morning, the SUV had not moved. A body slouched in the driver's seat, asleep. After brewing coffee, Hope covered up in a bathrobe and ball cap and plucked the newspaper from her doorstep, exposing only her forearm.

For the second consecutive day, her chin was front-page news. The *Chi-Town Tribune* had reprinted the *Mile-Hi Post* photo. She glanced at the reporter's name – not Paige Walker. *This story is too big for you, Half-a-Crouton,* she thought, before spotting her own name in print – Hope Allday. An anonymous neighbor had outed her and provided a quote: "She arrived home yesterday afternoon. No sign of Mr. Compatibility though." The article closed with George's poem, now reconstructed, everything but the last line:

Those eyes of yours
and that smile
and that heart –
that wonderful, didn't-see-it-coming,
knock-me-on-my-butt-while-stranded-in-DIA heart;
Your heart –
filled with all things worth exploring;
So long have I waited to see just this …

WHAT DID HE WHISPER NEXT?

"In anyone," mouthed Hope. Twenty-four hours had now passed without a word from George. No one was more ill-suited for prolonged silences than Hope, even when it was within the parameters of proper dating etiquette. Twenty-four hours. The passage of time was not insignificant. The feel of his lips had begun to recede.

Chapter 19

There were two SUVs out front now, four eyes on Hope's condo. The pappi from the previous night emerged from his vehicle. He flipped up the collar on his wool coat and scratched a stubbled cheek. The newcomer joined him. He tugged a beanie over his ears, handed coffee to his counterpart then fumbled for a cigarette. Both taller than average, they looked like Frost Giants, puffing while exchanging words, two predators on the shore of expectation. They braved the cold several minutes before retreating to idling vehicles. Daylight crept over the horizon, casting rays across a topless sky. Now two telephoto lenses pointed at Hope's front door.

Couldn't you sniff me out tomorrow? she thought, glaring through the blinds. She longed to feel the sunshine slanting through her window, warming her back while she sipped coffee and worked the crossword. Her goldfish stared blankly at her. "So this is what life in the aquarium is like, huh boys?" she said. "Not if I can help it."

An hour later, Hope ducked out her back door and scampered across the parking lot in Jackie Kennedy chic – knee-length trench coat, gray dress, scarf-bundled head, hand shielding her face, eyes darting behind Versace sunglasses. The absence of backdoor pappis surprised her.

April shoved open the passenger door of her Volkswagen Bug and gunned the accelerator the instant Hope buckled in. "Now *this* is living!" she shouted.

Hope scrambled for the handrail. "*What* are you doing?!?"

"Living! Un-muffle. You'll hear better. I know. Scarves score points with the fashion gods. Still. You won't catch me embalming my pretty little head like that." Seeing no cars trailing her, she eased off the gas pedal and rolled into Chicago's West Loop.

They found a coffee shop tucked away near *The Art Institute*. Hope un-scarfed and cradled a macchiato. She recounted the previous week, twisting her hair, checking text messages. The kiss felt surreal again when she described it, like another one of her dreams. Like Picasso doodle fish lived in that world, not real people. Reliving George's goodbye left her hair in tousles, looking like it needed to be scarfed again.

Such displays were a rarity. Order permeated Hope's world – from the meticulously clipped bonsai trees in her windowsills, to the precise angles of her furniture, to the nine goldfish populating her aquarium. Nine. Not eight. Not seven. Nine – the Oriental number of fulfillment. When one expired, it was immediately scooped out, flushed and replaced, preserving the number's integrity. She obsessed less over her goldfish than her personal appearance. Public outings meant perfect makeup, perfect outfits, perfect accessories, perfect hair. If it wasn't perfect, it didn't go out the door. Even more so of late, since becoming the Unmatchables' role model. Except now. Three hairs dangled across her brow – lost and flapping as the ventilation cycled on.

"You'll see him tomorrow, right?" asked April. "Tomorrow. Monday. The office?"

"Oh right. Monday – like a mafia hit, dressed in ugly, all unholy," replied Hope, muttering lines from an old poem. "Resuming the employer-employee relationship. That happens tomorrow morning. After sucking face over the weekend. Hadn't thought of that. Should be *gobs* of fun. Not awkward at all."

"You could call in sick."

Hope tried picturing the morning to come. *Liz, Mary and – heaven help me – Ted! And what if I see George? What will I say?* He still had not called. "Or I could call in dead. What if he doesn't call? How do you let go of perfect?"

"Perfect?" When Hope ran relationship diagnostics, she never arrived at perfect. Not even with her old flame Peter, the one she prematurely dubbed her "last first kiss." At present, no grounding words came to April. Even if they had, she knew that Hope would not permit her outside voice in. April empathized with reticence, like she did when Peter's true colors surfaced: Peter – the art major, tall, dark and color coordinated. Peter – turtlenecks, t-shirts and skinny jeans, every inch of fabric clinging to his wiry, vegan frame. His dimples and diamond stud earring blinded Hope to all that glared. Peter painted the human body in broad, confident strokes. He had a keen eye for the right light and, as Hope later discovered, women on the side. She lost something of herself in Peter, principally the ability to trust, and a playfulness. Losing George would be worse, April knew.

Hope sniveled on, now exercising potential George relationship scenarios aloud, sticking on the one in which he never again kissed her.

As the sun descended, April returned Hope to her condo. "Hey," said April. "Last time I checked, my phone still works. You know me: I'll be up late, even if I am asleep."

That night, before drifting off, Hope whispered, "Now I lay me down to stare at the ceiling and re-examine my life to this point." She had only one dream that night: *Blue Eyes* working the information booth again, translating Dutch poetry into English at the tulip festival. Only this time *Blue Eyes* was clearly George. April was right: Tulips weren't flowers. He kissed her repeatedly. Though unconscious, everything within her felt whole again. Aligned. Perfect.

The next morning, when Hope walked out the front door, cameras clicked like gun fire. She had forgotten about the pappis. Scampering to her car, she turned the ignition and sped away. A dozen more pappis awaited her in the Hancock Center lobby. Only this time, she spotted them through the windows before entering the building. *Let's just get this over with,* she thought, pushing the revolving glass door. Stepping forward, she drew strength from her red floaty dress, matching stilettos and white leather jacket.

Flashes blinded her path forward. "Any more poems from George over the weekend?" one photographer shouted. "Did you take the Compatibility Test? Is that how you found each other?"

Hope zeroed in on her feet until Mac appeared, like a dispatched angel. He halted the cabal with an extended arm, permitting only Hope through. "Gentlemen!" he snapped. "And I use the term liberally. Have ye no dignity? Cease and desist! Go home. Rethink yerselves before I snatch those bloody cameras and thump the lot of ye with 'em!"

"Where did they round up the goat herder?" chortled one pappi. He hoisted his camera over Mac's head and fired away. Others followed suit.

"I'm serious, fellas!" snarled Mac. "Deadly!" He took one threatening step forward before retreating inside the elevator just as the doors closed.

"Thank you," squeaked Hope.

"A pleasure. Glad ye made 'er home intact. The 'ol Celtic charm never fails."

"Oh. I forgot to bring it. I don't think I would have survived last week without it. Could have used it today as a matter of fact. No idea how I'll survive the next eight hours."

"Ye shall because ye must, like the rest of us. All ye' really have to do is make 'er to yer office, right? Ye can do that, miss. Hole up in there. Close the door. Shut out the world till quittin' time. I won't even pester ye about running up t'the top t'day."

"I'd be lost without you, Mac." Hope gave him a squeeze when the elevator stopped, then trudged down the hallway.

All eyes fell upon her as she entered the Love by George corporate suite. Stiff salutations followed, from Half-a-Donut Mary, Madeline and Sam, before fading into background whispers. Hal, the company attorney, tracked her movements, but said nothing.

Only Liz seemed herself. "Sooo, not a bad weekend, huh?" she began, slipping her arm through Hope's, escorting her to her office. "I had a feeling about George, only with me of course. I'll get over it. Maybe. You're an upgrade from that Paige creature. Start from the beginning. I want to be all hot and bothered by the end. And don't forget the poem. Loved that. I want to know how it ends. Then we can discuss the kissing. Not a day goes by that I don't fantasize about planting one on the boss."

Hope kept her mouth shut.

"Oh, I see how it is," groaned Liz. "Hal made you sign a non-disclosure agreement or something, didn't he? Nothing around this place surprises me anymore. Not with that worm yanking George's strings. You can't hold all this in, girl. It isn't natural. You'll get ulcers or high cholesterol or eat yourself into a coma. C'mon. I'm safe. Give up your secrets."

"Bathroom!" exclaimed Hope, breaking Liz's grip.

"Don't bathroom me!" hollered Liz. "We're not through here!"

Hope fled. Break room buzz spilled into the hallway. Ted's voice drowned out all others. "She should just shut up and sing! But mostly just shut up."

What's the name of that TV singing show they watch? she wondered. *At least they aren't talking about me.* She thrust open the bathroom door and locked herself in the corner stall, determined to wait out Liz. After disinfecting, she sat and counted down the ten minutes until the billing department's Monday morning meeting began.

It was day three of Georgelessness. A significant day. "If you don't hear from your date right away, don't sweat it," she had told the Unmatchables. "Silence could mean a number of things."

"Like how stupid I was to think I had a chance?" sneered Betty. "Or wait. You're a glass-half-full type, huh? Okay. Maybe he died. Better? That works for me. Why should anyone else have him if I can't, right?"

"*Not* exactly where I was going with this," Hope had replied. "Contact even after three days could still mean interest, reserved perhaps, you know, avoiding the appearance of being overly eager. Or maybe your date was just that busy – with work, family, previous enga …"

"And what if it's been five days?" trembled Margaret.

Hope put an arm around her. No need to say what they both knew: Five days was a clear rejection, anything after three actually.

Resurrection Day, Hope now thought. *Either he makes contact today or ….*

The break room was empty when Hope skirted past it again. Before shutting the door to her office, she recalled Mac's counsel and slipped the DO NOT DISTURB/IN A MEETING sign over the knob. She then checked emails: 218 new messages, one from George, time-stamped 10:06 a.m. Sunday morning. Addressed to all employees, it read:

I am out of town attending meetings this week. If you need a management decision, please contact Ted. Happy New Year! ~ G

Out of town? puzzled Hope. *What happened to needing a handler? That he can't be left alone after his accident? Is this his way of dusting me?*

She swiveled in her chair. Her eyes fell to the pedestrians and automobiles below, both stifled, it appeared, by an incoming mist. Swiveling back, she checked her voice mail. Nothing from George.

About noon-ish, she contemplated tackling her next Unmatchable class lesson plan and considered a trip to the mail room – tasks that needing doing. Instead she picked up the phone. *No!* she thought, hanging up. *Follow-up calls are a man's work, if he is any sort of man at all.*

The only knock on her door came mid-afternoon. *Coffee run? Is HE here?* wondered Hope, her heart skipping.

"Everything okay in there?" Liz voice thundered.

"Fine. Can't talk now."

What remained of the afternoon, she lost staring out the windows again. Overhead, a thickening cloud canopy compressed the sky's ceiling, permitting only a shadow of sunlight through – the last remnant of the Day after Christmas Blizzard according to the weather report. At straight up 5:00 p.m., quitting time, Hope folded her arms on her desk, buried her head and sobbed. *Alone again, in a world made for couples.*

Chapter 20

Ted choked on his coffee after picking up the *Tribune* off his porch and seeing: CHICAGO'S MOST ELIGIBLE BACHELOR IN LOVE? "Well that's just *freaking* perfect!" he bellowed, wiping his chin with the sleeve of his bathrobe. He glared at the full-color image of the kiss, slammed the door and punched the keys on his cell phone. "Morning, Hal," he seethed, ignoring the hello on the other end. "I know. Time and a half today. No need to say it. Love by George conference room. One hour."

He closed his eyes and counted down from ten, then dialed George. "Why are you ruining my Sunday?"

"Well, top of the morning to you, Ted," replied George. "I'd ask how you are, perhaps comment about the weather, you know, like civilized people do, but why bother? What is it now?"

"Oh nothing much. Just the end of your career. Front page of the *Trib.* Go ahead. Take a peek. Next time, have the *decency* to give me a heads up."

"Decency? *You* are lecturing *me* about decency?"

Ted seethed. "Hal and I will be at the office in an hour coordinating *your* damage control. Might be a good idea if you showed up."

Click.

"Decency!" repeated George, typing the *Trib*'s URL on his laptop. Minutes later, he drove straight to the office. Unchecked, he knew that Ted and Hal would craft some knee-jerk response to the harmless news coverage. It might even be helpful. Might attract new clients. But Ted and Hal always planned for the worst, a natural extension, it seemed, of their personalities. They would need to be reined in.

"Meeting number 561!" announced George when he appeared in the conference room, slamming down his notebook on the table. "Here's a prediction: Total waste of time." He sat down, clicked a ballpoint pen and wrote: "MEETING #561. ATTENDEES: me and the brain trust."

Ted pushed the *Tribune* across the table and primed his jowls. He was in the act of not cursing. Decades ago, he had renounced profanity. Love for his wife had miraculously cleaned his tongue. That and Providence. "When tempted, try saying Jesus, Mary and the Holy Saint Joseph instead," advised Ted's priest when the non-profanity began. "If offered sincerely, it's a prayer, not a curse." Right now, the urge to pray in George's face consumed him.

"Yeah. I read it. And?" said George. "So I just had a little fun. People do that. If they didn't, we wouldn't have a business. Why is this a crisis?"

Silence.

"What?" asked George. "Why are you two looking at me like that? Say something. And sit down, would you? Gives me the creeps when you two hover."

"What part of sexual harassment don't you understand?" replied Ted, pulling up a chair.

"Sexual harassment?" laughed George. He shoved the paper back across the table and pointed to the photo. "That's absurd. The feeling, as you can see, was mutual."

"*But* you are her boss," countered Ted. "I thought you were smarter than this. Enlighten him would you, Hal?"

"If she doesn't lawyer up by the week's end, no one will be more stunned than I," said Hal, a former trial lawyer who preferred standing. He strolled to the window – wafting the smell of pipe tobacco from his trademark black suit. He stroked his white goatee, his eyes settling beyond the horizon to a courtroom of his imaginings. "Alleged unwanted advances. Alleged pervasiveness. Boss does nothing to stop it, *allegedly.* She tilts her head, squeezes out tears on the witness stand. Pretty young thing. Soft brown eyes. She says, 'If I didn't return my boss's affections, I feared losing my job. And now I can't go anywhere without having my privacy invaded – photographers, the general public, everyone. My life is a circus.' It's a slam dunk. We *might* settle out of court for six digits if we are lucky."

Ted guffawed. "There's a big if, not to mention the business fallout. Clients will dump Love by George in droves. Who wants dating services from a sexual harasser?"

George threw his head back and stared at the ceiling. "I am *not* a sexual harasser."

"Irregardless," said Ted. "The accusation is all that matters."

"Not a word," George corrected. "Follow along now: regardless, meaning without regard. Therefore irregardless would mean …?"

"Fine! Don't take this seriously!" Ted fired back. "Jesus, Mary and the Holy Saint Joseph! What's the matter with you? If you're going to waste my time, I'll just go home."

"Finally, we're getting somewhere."

Ted glared back. "Try following *this* for just one minute: You will be tried by a jury of your peers, found guilty of having deep pockets and pay dearly. *Your bank roll* is on trial here, not my vocabulary. Think suck bucket dribble drain."

"Zero contact with Hope," Hal broke in. "And zero means zero. No phone calls. No emails. No texts. Not a peep. Madeline is now Hope's boss. And *you* are going away until we see what Hope's next move is."

"I can't do that," objected George. Ted's reddening face now stirred his compassion. *I know, buddy. You're trying to help. Okay. Let's assume for one minute that you aren't overreacting. That Hope isn't who she appears to be. I can't risk losing it all now, not when I'm this close.* Truth was that George could have retired long ago, but a larger goal prevented it. Just a few million more in the bank would be enough for Ted – unaware of George's scheme – to retire too. And Madeline. And Half-a-Donut Mary. And Mac. Plus a windfall for a few other worthy souls. It was simple math. Soon, everyone that mattered would be set for life. That was the plan – now within sight, only a year or two away. A far superior plan than leaving their retirement to the whims of the stock market. No bona fide Leo with George's means could resist such a display of fierce loyalty. Abby was his first beneficiary. She was now spending every day with her grandkids, no longer worried about money. It had been George's best investment. He would stay the course to see the rest of his peeps spend their days in comfort.

"I'm not *asking* you to go away," continued Hal. "I'm *telling* you. I don't want to see you here for at least a couple of weeks. After the dust settles, we reassess. *Regardless*, a few things must change. From here on out, you can never again take disciplinary action on Hope. Nor can you fire her. Or offer criticism. She skates on everything. And she must be considered for every promotion, even if she's unqualified. I want a paper trail demonstrating that you bent over backward to be nondiscriminatory. Got it? If in doubt, call me."

"Discipline?" repeated George. "Unqualified? *She* could run this company." He recounted Hope's commercial ideas and her suggestion to expand Love by George to include married couples' services. "And that, gentlemen, is why I doubled her salary. She is far from unqualified."

"Doubled it?" gnarled Ted.

Hal trailed off again into reverie. "Then again, is a supervisor one with disciplinary powers to transfer or fire an employee? or per *Vance v. Ball State University*, someone potentially liable for indirect oversight?"

In the half hour that followed, George fleshed out the possibility of what Hal dubbed a "consensual dating agreement" – a magical piece of employer-employee legalese akin to a prenuptial agreement. "A consensual agreement *might* protect your assets if you continue seeing her, but only if it stipulates that you engage in dating activities outside of the work environment," explained Hal. "However, I do not recommend it."

"I say he who signs the paychecks gets the final word," replied George. "Draw up the agreement. I'll grant you one week, not two, gentlemen, to figure out how to mitigate any additional financial risk that you think I've put the company in. I'll consent to Madeline being Hope's boss for the time being. But in seven days, I'll be calling Hope for pleasure, not business. Plan accordingly."

It was Hal who crafted the company email announcing George's absence – the one that Hope lamented the next day in her office. While Hal parsed words, George busied himself with travel arrangements – Hawaii this time, more specifically Mauna Kea's 13,792-foot peak. Hawaii was one of the few remaining states on the rock collecting to-do list. For years, he had anticipated its summit – bleach-white snow and tholeiitic basalt rock. Now the pursuit ahead felt like a consolation prize – one lacking color. No ravenous red. No wildly conflicted purple. No brunette trusses worth running his fingers through. But he had given Ted and Hal his word. And so, ten minutes later, he drove to O'Hare.

After buckling into his seat, he tugged a new ball cap over his brow. Hal's words returned to him – no calling, no emails, no texts, no nothing. *Why did I agree to that?* His eyes drifted across the aisle to a white smear on the nearest armrest: creamer. A pony-tailed blonde occupied the seat. She flitted through a fashion magazine, sipping coffee, oblivious to the spill. *Well, she's no Hope*, thought George. The dribble would require two sanitizing wipes to properly eradicate – a fact he would not have known only a week ago. *Seven more days without sanitizing wipes. That's too long.*

Back in Chicago, Hope continued to spiral.

Tuesday was more insufferable than Monday. Fewer pappis lurked, though, only two that she spotted on her way to work. The condo pappis had departed. That morning, one tabloid published the hotel bed sheet story in startling detail. "Clean ones!" Hope read in print, her name attributed to the quote. *Aaand there goes my dignity again,* she thought. The PR prompted one inquiry.

"Sniffing inhalants now? People die from that, you know," her mother admonished on the telephone. "Candles of all things. I raised you better. Of course I would be *the last* to know if you died. The way you ignore me, you might as well not even have a mother. Do you know how many messages I left over the weekend? I called you at home, no answer. Called you on your cell phone, no answer. Texted. Emailed. No answer, no answer, no answer."

Hope offered no rebuttal. She spent Wednesday holed up in her office again. The DO NOT DISTURB/IN A MEETING sign remained on her doorknob. On Thursday afternoon, April called. "You don't have to go through this alone," she said. "I'm safe. Lean on me."

Friday arrived without even a trickle of optimism. What was there to look forward to? More thinking? More time to lament George's vanishing? His disinterest. At least at work Hope had one mandatory distraction: her first Unmatchables class of the New Year. How she would survive standing before them in her present state, she did not know.

As usual, Mac escorted her up the elevator that morning. About half way there, "The Love Boat" theme song (the ring tone she had assigned George) played. Mac peeked over at Hope as she dug through her handbag. "Hello?" she answered, butterflies swarming. "George?"

No reply – only indistinguishable chatter, though George's tone was unmistakable. A second background voice sounded familiar, despite Hope's inability to identify it. *Is he covering the mouthpiece?* she wondered. The muted conversation continued until only one explanation remained: George had inadvertently called, possibly butt dialed. The proper thing to do, of course, was to hang up and respect his privacy. But how could she? She hadn't heard his voice in a week. Her body ached at the sound of it. *Where is he?* she wondered, straining to hear. *Who is he talking to?* She could not distinguish words until stepping off the elevator.

"*No one* could be happier than me," said George, his voice now clear. "Truly."

Happier about what? wondered Hope. She placed the phone in her handbag as she neared the front door, planning to listen again from her office. Then she looked up.

Scarcely a dozen feet away, through the "Love by George" glass door, every question was answered. With the billing department gathered, Paige embraced George and laughed, steadying a cloche hat with one hand. "Oh, Georgie!" she beamed. "I'm the luckiest girl in the world!" Clinging to him (his back was facing the door), Paige spotted Hope. With a nod, she extended her arm, revealing the largest diamond ring Hope that had ever seen, then blew a condescending kiss.

The color abandoned Hope's face as her mind strained for a single coherent thread. *George and ... her!*

Paige nodded again, savoring Hope's comeuppance.

George followed Paige's eyes. "Hope!" he exclaimed. He released Paige and reached toward the glass.

Clasping her mouth with a hand, Hope scampered down the hallway.

"Hope! Hope!" she heard George shout. A run of footsteps followed until the elevator doors shut behind her, and she felt herself descending.

"I'm ... I'm ... done here," she sniveled to Mac, drawing a deep breath.

Mac pressed the emergency stop button and gathered her in his arms. She sobbed until exhausting her tears, then phoned Madeline and whimpered, "I quit." Afterward, she reached in her handbag for a cigarette that was not there.

Chapter 21

It's fate, thought Hope, her tears blurring the drive home. What else could it be? Life's winners spoke of destiny, not fate. Meanwhile, fate coldly rationed happiness for people like Hope, life's ordinary creatures. *Stupid! – thinking that I could contend with Paige's charms! Why can't I remember the look on George's face instead? Duped again - this time with a poem and a kiss. Stupid! – allowing yourself to feel. There is no cheating fate.*

"But it was *my* eyes, *my* smile, *my* heart," sniffled Hope when she stomped through the door of her condo. She tossed her keys and handbag on the coffee table, nosedived into the couch and beat her pillows. "I inspired poetry. Me! Not …"

The Love Boat theme song filled the air again. Lifting her head, blinking through tears, she picked up her phone, incredulous to see George's name on the display. "NOW you want to talk? When the past calls, it never has anything useful to say."

A hot bath. That's what I need now, not this, she thought. Steam, bubbles, essential oils and lotions. If only she could wipe Paige from her consciousness. Paige and now George's voicemail chime. *Don't listen to it,* she thought while finishing her soak and toweling off. She clicked on the TV.

Trumpets blasted. All nine goldfish retreated to the back of the tank. A history of the English monarchy was in progress. "… shortly thereafter, King George III developed porphyria," said the narrator, "a disease marked by abdominal pain, muscle weakness, vomiting, depression, anxiety, hallucinations and paranoia. He died deaf, blind and in a state of madness."

Another George the Third who married without Hope! Fate! Ugh!

She retreated to the kitchen and found relief in the back of the freezer. *Ice cream before noon. A new low.* She then dug out her portable TV/DVD player from the hall closet and began a cinematic detox – a battery of movies, all romances, that Hope watched in succession when relationships fizzled. How she ached to experience the on-screen magic – blind leaps inspired then taken, hearts discovered and aligned, somedays seized and never relinquished.

First up in "The Rock-Bottom Suite" was *You've Got Mail.* With the vanilla ripple tub resting on her chest and the TV/DVD player on the step stool in front of her, Hope sat with crisscrossed legs on the kitchen tile. The opening credits appeared like old friends. Harry Nilsson crooned *"The Puppy Song."* Chasing ice cream with coffee, she settled on the living room couch and weathered the first happy ending:

Joe Fox (Tom Hanks): "Don't cry shop girl."
Kathleen Kelly (Meg Ryan): "I wanted it to be you... wanted it to be you so badly."
The long overdue kiss.
"Somewhere over the Rainbow" played.

"They just don't make movies like that anymore," blubbered Hope, destroying several Kleenexes. She then popped in *Sleepless in Seattle* and watched it straight through, mouthing the ending's words "shall we." True love walked off hand-in-hand into a future she long imagined.

She played movie number three straightaway – *Pride and Prejudice,* the six-hour mini-series – and found a bag of potato chips, fried, not baked. Real chips. Real, not imaginary taste. Ten grams of fat per serving. She munched until bloating and felt no guilt. Two TUMS later, she retired to bed – nestling under the covers, sitting with her back to the headboard, the TV/DVD player now at her side. Everything felt cozy again until Miss Carolyn Bingley spoke:

"No woman can be really esteemed accomplished, who does not also possess a certain something in her air, in her manner of walking, in the tone of her voice, her address and expressions."

Nooo! Don't do this to me, Bingley! thought Hope, who had recited the lines aloud countless times, mocking. Only this time, Miss Bingley wasn't funny. She took on Paige's voice. Had the same look in her eye. Morphed before her eyes into a modern-day incarnation. Bingley and Paige were one and the same. Only their fates differed: Miss Bingley, a selfish, conceited antagonist failed in her ungoverned wiles. Paige did not. Paige had George.

Hope hit the pause button, hating the face on screen – condescending, on the verge of blowing another mocking kiss at her. *Stealing George wasn't enough for you, Paige?* thought Hope. *Now you've poisoned my movie rotation!* She cried herself to sleep.

The next morning, Hope attempted to resume *Pride and Prejudice*, but lasted only 10 seconds. She contemplated skipping it, but knew that the next movie – *Sense and Sensibility*, another Jane Austen romance – would also be ruined. Paige would most certainly morph herself into another character. Skipping ahead to *Return to Me* was out of the question. It would only double the hole in the suite, undermining the therapeutic value of the entire exercise.

i shall never again watch p&p or s&s, apes, she texted – a declaration akin to the rest of humanity renouncing oxygen.

April responded in person, pounding on Hope's door, waiting for an answer slow in coming. "I know you're in there!"

Hope turned the bolt and cracked open the door. She peeked out through red, puffy eyes, hair in a ponytail, no makeup.

"You could use some company," said April. Stepping inside, she shut the door then presented a macchiato. They walked to the living room. *Pride & Prejudice* was still paused on screen.

"How worried should I be?"

Hope shook her head. "I'm fine."

"No more Pride and Prejudice? No more Sense and Sensibility? I thought I would find a corpse in here after reading that."

Hope choked out the story of George's engagement.

April hugged and held and said nothing. Afterward, she disappeared in the kitchen and emerged with two steaming bowls of chicken noodle soup. She placed them on the dining room table. But for a few slurps, they soup-ed in silence. Then April removed an envelope from her Gucci bag and presented it. "Here: This won't fix relationships, but it might help with your other dreams."

Hope glanced at it. "What is this?"

"A royalty check. $2,000 worth."

"Royalty check?" repeated Hope, picking it up, opening it with her index finger. "For what?"

"Remember that idea you said I could have – The Stupid Gong. You said it wasn't worth pursuing. Well, a funny thing happened. I got it patented – in your name of course – then hired a manufacturer. I had three hundred made. I built a website, pitched a few retailers, and bang! Sold out. There are more back orders than I can fill. So last week I sold the patent. Well, technically you did." She slid a second envelope in front of Hope. The check inside was ten times the amount of the first.

"Huh?" Hope stared back, after opening it, bewildered.

April reached across the table and squeezed her hand. "Remember that dream of yours: owning a coffee shop and writing poetry? No more dreaming about it now. You get royalties every time someone buys a gong. Oh. I've also got a patent lawyer checking into your "That Was Stupid" button idea. I have a feeling that lightning could strike twice. Speaking of dreams, I have one that's share-worthy: I was at your house. Only it wasn't this place. It was a mansion. You feng shui-ed every square foot. Anyway, I was going from room to room, calling your name, trying to find you. Yes, I was sleepwalking. No, I didn't injure myself. I woke up in my pantry holding a can of caviar. Anyway, the place in the dream, your mansion, was so big that I couldn't even find you. I think it means something."

I have money, mused Hope when April departed. *I don't have to work. How long can this possibly last?* Her mind reviewed the milestones that lead to this moment: valedictorian of her high school class, partial scholarship to the University of Tampa, marine biology degree/minor in poetry, a failed greeting card venture, Love by George, now this development: mastermind behind the Stupid Gong.

Good news never felt so hollow.

No news could fill the vacuum left by George. The best that she could now hope for was for him to look back someday with regret, consumed by his own *what if –* someday when he was on his yacht putting distance between himself and his pill of a wife.

What is it like to be him? Hope tried imagining, *to have anyone you want? To be the one impossible to get over?* She wandered to the living room, picked her cell phone up from the coffee table and turned it back and forth in her hand. *I still have his voice mail. But will I ever hear his voice again in person? Wait! Doesn't the law require employers to issue a final paycheck within 24 hours of an employee demanding it? Even if I wasn't fired?*

The ruse – credible, albeit desperate – would afford her an epilogue. Maybe *she could* return to the office Monday and permit George one final glimpse of what he would be missing out on the rest of his life. She could then take a mental snapshot of his reaction and begin coping. *Ulcers will be hatched,* she thought, picturing it, suddenly feeling repurposed.

When Monday morning arrived, Hope dolled up in militant detail. After the final spritz, she took a step backward and assessed. The looking glass did not lie. *Woof!*

Before walking out the door, she read the *Tribune* horoscope: "Today is a tumultuous five. Yield to the current, and you know what to expect. Heed your inner voice. Weather the tide, and the prize will be worth the price."

"Worth every penny," she sneered.

Chapter 22

No bolder chin had ever shone than the one that Hope presented at the Love by George reception desk. It bore no resemblance to the quivering, drippy mess not 72 hours prior, when Paige bewitched the lobby with the rock on her finger. But this chin! It was the focal point of a posture resolute – a hip thrust forward, a hand atop its crest, the other hand on the counter. The sight arrested all speech. Adding machines fell silent. Eyes peeked over cubicles. Only the faint melody of mood music remained unaltered: *"Love-uh-uh-uh-of-ing you … sooo easy … you're sooo beautiful …."*

"I am here for my paycheck," announced Hope. She slapped the counter and surveyed her audience. *Where's George? Ted? Madeline? Mary? Hal?* she wondered. Only Karli and the accounting department ogled back with expressions ranging from pity to shock. *George is supposed to be looking at me like that!*

"Your paycheck?" stammered Karli. Her eyes bulged into hazel question marks.

What a waste of a perfect entrance! thought Hope. *Not a single soul from administration to witness it.* "My *last* paycheck," she intoned. "Ring Madeline, please. Inform her that I would like my paycheck this instant."

"Rrright" Karli pressed Madeline's extension. "Hi. Um, *Hope* is at the front desk. Yes, right here. She wants her final paycheck. Uh huh. Uh huh. Oh." She opened her desk drawer. "Oh. Thanks." She hung up. With a cringe, she offered Hope an envelope. "I guess they were expecting you."

Snatching it from Karli's hand, Hope tore it open. It was no bluff. It was, indeed, her paycheck and a hand-written note from George that read:

Why are you are leaving? Why won't you answer my calls? Devastated! ~ G

Hope's eyes darted down the administrative wing. More silence. More mood music (same song). *"And la la la la la ..."*

Expecting me? marveled Hope, her mind in scrambles. *Whaaa? This is NOT how this is supposed to go down!* "Well, that *is* what I came for," she finally declared, salvaging a voice. Waving the check, she pointed over Karli's shoulder. "That and my things."

After storming off, she halted in the doorway of her office. Someone had stacked empty boxes next to her desk. *Not only did he expect me, he wants me gone.* She slammed the door and began packing, banging everything that wouldn't break. A note taped to her computer eventually silenced her:

Don't go. This feels all wrong. I don't want to lose you. Please call. ~ G

Hope crumpled it and threw it at the door, imagining George's body standing there, occupying the empty space. *Don't want to lose you, but here's your paycheck!* she thought. *Don't want to lose you, but here's some boxes to pack your things!* She yanked open the bottom desk drawer. Something wobbled. The smell of hotel bed sheets perfumed the air. *Stupid candle!* She wiped away a tear, kicked the drawer shut and exited her office clutching only her paycheck. Resolute, she pounded her heels down the administrative wing.

Where is he? she wondered, her pace quickening. *Time for YOU to wet yourself, Mr. Devastated! Mr. Don't Want to Lose You! Mr. ... where are you?* Every office was dark. She halted at the end of the corridor and spun around. At last, she spotted warm bodies – all huddled around the executive meeting room table: Ted, Hal, Madeline and Mary. They stared back, all eyebrows. George's chair was vacant. *Well that's just perfect!* thought Hope. After one spiteful salute, she resumed her stride, breezing past the front counter and right out the door. *Don't look back. Ever!*

She half-expected to find another note from George taped to the elevator. Instead, she found Mac, squirming over her composure. He pressed the ground floor button. Together, they stared ahead in silence, watching the elevator doors closing until a set of plump fingers thrust between them. The fingers grew into a hand, then an arm, then a pear-shaped body in a navy pinstriped suit. Ted!

"Hope," he wheezed, stepping inside. "Wasn't sure when I'd see you again."

She dug through her handbag and addressed Mac. "Here." She placed his Celtic charm in the palm of his hand then folded his fingers over it. "Thanks for everything. *You, sir,* are a true gentleman. Not many of you left these days. One fewer this week than last by my count."

Ted cleared his throat. "Quite a snowstorm there in Denver. Not entirely a waste of time though, from what I hear. But now you are leaving us. What a shame."

Hope glared. "Perhaps the joy of interviewing my replacement will dull your pain."

"Replacement?" laughed Ted. "Rest assured, my dear, *you* are not replaceable. But don't you worry about us. We'll manage somehow. Of course, I'll have to keep a closer eye on George. He'll probably paint another nightmare now."

"What is *that* supposed to mean?"

"Exactly what it implies, I imagine. You will be missed. Oh! Before *I* forget, good call on the love lottery ad. We discussed it in staff this morning. We plan to shoot it next week, matter of fact. Thought you'd like to know. And your other idea – about offering relationship services to married couples – thumbs up on that too. You know, I liked you right from the start. Which reminds me." He lifted a pant leg, revealing a beige and navy argyle sock. "Get a load of these chick magnets."

Hope's brow twitched.

"Anyway, it's a shame losing you," continued Ted, "after we're just now getting cozy. People: what a crap shoot! Oh well. Let me know if you need a letter of recommendation."

"Sounds like everyone in this dysfunctional little family is going to be just fine!" snapped Hope. "Except me, of course. Sucks to be me! Tell me: Did George put you up to this, or was it Hal? Who crafted this narrative? I can't believe they trusted you with *this* tap dance. Your elevator appearance has nothing to do with well wishing."

"It wasn't the sole purpose. If you must know, I was headed to the coffee shop. I had a hankering."

"Hankering! To catch *this* elevator you had to sprint!" snapped Hope. "C'mon! *You are here* to make sure that what happened Denver stays in Denver. It's optics. You are damage control. Here to make nicey nice. You of all people! How unnatural for you! Can't risk me airing my dirty laundry. That would be bad for business. Well, no need to lose sleep over it. I am not *completely* deficient of virtue. That makes one of us. You can tell George and Hal that I don't kiss and tell. I'm not that kind of girl."

"How 'bout a quick dash t'the top then?" interjected Mac. He had been quietly texting on his phone. "Could be your last chance."

Hope's eyes widened, then narrowed, turning from Mac to Ted again. He shared her fear of elevators. She punched the emergency stop and hit the 100th floor button. "Let's dance, Marbles!"

Expressionless, Ted searched his pockets. He extracted a plastic vial, twisted the cap and swallowed a tablet. "Motion sickness pills," he explained. "I can go all day, Sweetheart!"

"Ugh!" Hope fumbled for the handrail and felt her breath turn shallow. When the elevator dinged to a stop, she stumbled through the parting doors. "Oof!" she uttered, colliding into a random body, a male by the feel of things. She latched onto sleeved forearms and drove the muscular frame into the carpeting. *That smell!* thought Hope, as she lay atop him, disoriented. *You've got to be kidding me! George!* "You!" she screeched, scrambling to her feet. "So this is where you've been hiding?"

"It *is* her!" a woman in the crowd proclaimed. "The poetry tutor. And look! George Springs!"

Wincing, George stood and braced his back. "That's gonna' leave a mark."

Hope's pulse quickened at the sight of him. And the smell. And the feel. It took every ounce of restraint within her to refrain from helping him to his feet. "And what about the permanent mark you left on me?" she fumed instead, picking up a broken heel. Parting the crowd, she hobbled to the nearest window. Fog had rolled in, settling just below the top floor. It concealed the Lake Michigan shoreline and the surrounding high-rises. Only Willis Tower conquered the mist, poking above it like a castle keep on a medieval morning.

"Hope," implored George, inching forward. "I tried to call."

Hope's eyes riveted on the tower. "Just go find Paige."

"It's you I need," said George, his voice nearer now. "I am not a needy person, but I need you."

"Need me for commercial ideas. Need me to fix the Unmatchables. Need me when you are bored and stranded. Sorry. Not playing along anymore."

George reached into his breast pocket, opened an envelope, extracted a greeting card and spoke:

"No alarms -
clocks or sirens,
that someday imagined;
Just your touch –
the feel of it!
And the naked concern
in your eyes;
I am lost

in the palpable contents
of a heart opened wide ...'

You left me hanging with that. Well, after no small effort, I tracked the card down in a gift store. You shouldn't have stopped there.

'Let me,' you say,
fluffing pillows,
warming my cup,
steeping my insides;
You fuss with my covers
until they are right
and kiss my forehead
because ...'"

"I know how it ends," snapped Hope, raising a palm, her cold shoulder growing colder. She had intended to silence him long before, but could not. The power of his voice! – even now, probably forever. It weakened her. And he had read her poem with the same desperation from which it was penned. Such a sincere recitation deserved better than to be silenced, that is, until he reached the part about kissing, and she could bear it no more. "Don't! You'll have to find someone else to write commercials. Now please.... Just go!"

"Where? I want to be that guy in the greeting card."

Hope spun around. Cameras flashed. An audience had assembled and continued to grow. "Be that guy!" she repeated, wiping the corner of her eye. "Just one *itty bitty* problem. You're engaged."

The crowd jeered.

"It's a modern-day tragedy," one onlooker said. "What a jerk!"

"Is this where we put on our surprised faces?" mocked another. "I never bought that sad orphan shtick."

"I *knew* those commercials were too good to be true,"

another added. "Online romance! What piffle! People should just find love the old-fashioned way – at churches and in bars."

"Engaged?" repeated George.

"To Paige," said Hope in a broken tone. "I saw the ring. How could I not?"

"That's what this is about? Well, you're half right. *Paige* is engaged. *My* only engagement has been attempting to contact you. Thank goodness Mac delivered you here, otherwise I may never have succeeded. *What you saw* at the office last week was Paige announcing her engagement to Wilfred – a fine chap, rather ancient as fiancées go, but who am I to judge? His net worth surpasses mine – that's something – of course he's been at it much longer. It's you I'm interested in. You. Denver was the last time I felt alive. Last time since, I don't know. You're so much better with words than I am. Somewhere between Denver and Chicago, I got lost again. Lost because you weren't by my side. Was I the only one who felt that?"

Hope's gaze fell to George's lips. "You mean, you're not ...?"

George shook his head. "Not yet. I *was* starting to hope."

"Well, I guess that makes me your girl. But there's something I have to do first."

"I never know what is going to happen next when you say that."

Hope stepped forward then twisted and tugged on George's shirt button until ripping it off. "There! I wanted to do that last week. A life filled with regret is no life at all. Wrong shirt, but it will have to do."

Then, for the second time within the stretch of a week, she pulled down George's head, pressed up against his body and – broken heel and all – tippy toed her way up to his lips. Sunlight now slanted through the windows – piercing the fog, the skin and every spirit within the 100th floor – illuminating their mostly widely photographed kiss to date.

The crowd erupted.

"I say that we pick up right where we left off," said George a long while later. "Let's get out of here. Hop another plane, this time to someplace warm. How does dinner on a beach tonight sound?"

"Another airplane?" Hope relinquished his embrace.

"Well I can't do this alone. Who would disinfect if you didn't come? How about this time you pick the restaurants? I'll order the wine." He reached again for her. "C'mon, Dirtwad. I'll hold your hand. No need to pretend to check my mood ring anymore."

"I dunno. Could be risky," said Hope, placing her palm in his. "I might not let go."

"I don't want you to."

Ninety minutes later, they were on the tarmac. Just before takeoff, Hope posted a photo (on Facebook) of them kissing and captioned it:

Just like that it happened –
in bits and pieces
and parts made whole;
In turning a heart
inside out,
without even trying at all.

The End

Hope's Other Poems

(a sampling)

***

Just beneath the skin –
is a child dying to play,
is a heart unafraid,
is a thought I can't explain,
is a feeling I dare not say;
Just beneath the skin –
is me
only better.

***

It hit me just now
then escaped somehow
exactly as it came:
a flash, a reverie, then POOF!
suck bucket dribble drain;
I gave fierce chase –
a Sunday drive,
a shower long and hot,
an inked-up diner napkin,
all yielding zip, nary, not –
(but turkey bacon
and scrambled thought);
Assuming this breath
the next
and another
and boldness of chin –
it will come to me again;
What then?

***

***

The invisible between us –
clumsily spoken,
absolute,
unbroken;
Nothing is this perfect
except this.

***

Monday –
like a mafia hit,
dressed in ugly,
all unholy;
In steam rolls
empty toilet paper rolls
in unforeseen unknowables,
and midday meetings,
over inbox clutter,
and the re-scheduling two-step –
madness,
and yet we dance.

***

***

Grace –
penetrating the fog,
the skin,
the spirit within,
with something beyond
this outstretched hand.

***

To you!
– that you that you see
in the mirror,
in the blue moon,
when the inner critic
is tongue-tied
and exposed.

***

Psst!
Even in silence,
you are much company –
all I ever need.

***

***

Someday –
I will put my toes in the sand.
I will follow my heart.
I will write that novel.
I will make things right.
I will chase dreams.
And surrender.
Someday –
I will live.

***

Can't win if I don't play,
and you know I won't,
can't,
don't have it in me;
You know!
I know that you know –
that me
that you tragically know …
… at least for now,
or at most,
for now is all we know.

***

Rethink yourself –
as is,
without deficiency;
Add grins;
Add giggles.

***

***

Somewhere –
a lighthouse
on a bed of white,
bare feet and alive;
Hand-in-hand
with you,
my world,
my very air.

***

Almost missed
the peek show –
that clouded portal
breaking heaven
with a promise.

***

Once I was young and dumb
with shallow eyes;
Now I am older.

***

**

Do,
undo,
re-do
the Updo -
the flipped collars
and waxed brows,
the Lifestyle Lifts
and killer kicks;
The box seats,
and executive suites;
The faster L –
bigger,
better,
more baggage
in the now;
And more gravity -
there for the cheating
just once more,
and then again;
There I go –
fleeing
falling sand,
the mirror's math
and long looks back
I used to take,
in real time,
when last I held your hand.

**

**

(from Biology 101 class)

Sand hill crane –
stand all alone;
Strike a pose
Lord of the Pond,
Master of Scum;
Show some leg –
just that one,
just in case
company come.

**

Your give:
more revealing
than your take –
all ripples
and echoes.

**

I found something
at sea
and in the mountain
and got lost in between;
Time only for a cuppa' joe there,
perhaps;
For I am elsewhere –
in the surf and rock and grains
of things better felt than seen.

**

***

Not quite right
nor altogether wrong,
more of a plumb gray,
more visible with age.

***

A repartee for two –
me and you
~ canoodles ~
steeped and tossed
and left to stew.

***

Lost from sight –
done departed
out the window,
transparent
long ago;
Tragic,
that empty star,
wasting bling
on the blind,
dead to hope.

***

In whistles and puffs,
the Frost Giants come –
waylaying,
whitewashing,
canvassing the earth.

***

**

The inspired leap –
that someday seized,
when hearts discover
and align
and know.

**

Subterfuge and
Schadenfreude;
Slick shticks,
slapsticks
and serendipity doo.

**

Off to our own separate beaches
again,
1,000 miles apart –
deflating, wrinkling,
emptying with time.

**

She left the canvas wet
for outstretched hands and foreign lands,
a tulip in time –
bursting
inside out
from beyond,
speaking without a word
into the here and now
and ever more.

**

***

I must away
into the unknown
where I am more than a paycheck,
a footnote, a taker's trove,
to feel again
before it is too late,
and let the whisper
find a voice.

***

'Tis life,
that is all –
but a mist,
finite,
with soul.

***

SUSAN VOLK'S POEM
(Hope's coffee shop owner life coach –
www.mountaingrindwinterpark.com)

The compass
behind this breastbone
leads me places
I least expect to go.

***

List of State Peaks

(with George's notes)

STATE	*PEAK ELEV.*	*NAME*	*NOTES*
Alabama	2,413	Cheaha Mountain	a.k.a. "High Place," sandstone
Alaska	20,236	Mount McKinley	yet to be climbed
Arizona	12, 637	Humphrey's Peak	a.k.a. San Francisco Peak, igneous
Arkansas	2,753	Magazine Mountain	plateau, cliffs, dive-bombed by birds, sandstone
California	14,505	Mount Whitney	was only English-speaking hiker, granite
Colorado	14,440	Mount Elbert	lightning, mountain goat, marmot, quartzite
Connecticut	2,379	Mount Frissell	2-hour hike, steep, need new hiking boots
Delaware	447	Ebright Azimuth	road-side monument in developed area, yawn
Florida	345	Britton Hill	beat the hurricane, hilly, farms nearby
Georgia	4,784	Brasstown Bald	not truly bald, trees, can see Atlanta, soapstone
Hawaii	13,803	Mauna Kea	skied down in January! missing Hope, basalt
Idaho	12,668	Borah Peak	named for politician! used ice ax, above tree line

Illinois	1,235	Charles Mound	private land, < 1 mile from Wisconsin
Indiana	1,257	Hoosier Hill	private land, Ted joined. whiner! never again
Iowa	1,671	Hawkeye Point	marked by mosaic, locals hopped up on corn
Kansas	4,041	Mount Sunflower	plaque: "nothing happened here in 1897" – agree
Kentucky	4,145	Black Mountain	one-lane dirt road to summit, found piece of coal
Louisiana	535	Driskill Mountain	signed log book in lock box, quartz
Maine	5,270	Mount Katahdin	like a postcard, bull moose in velvet, granite
Maryland	3,360	Hoye-Crest	private land, nice view of Potomac River
Massachusetts	3,489	Mount Greylock	lighthouse-ish marker, 5 states visible, phyllite
Michigan	1,979	Mount Arvon	½ mile hike, signed log book in blue mailbox
Minnesota	2,302	Eagle Mountain	should call it mosquito mountain, saw no eagles
Mississippi	807	Woodall Mountain	a.k.a. Yow Hill, 1-mi. hike to summit
Missouri	1,772	Taum Sauk Mountain	did not find Tom's socks, shale
Montana	12,807	Granite Peak	Paige, porcupine, moose, hummed John Denver
Nebraska	5,427	Panorama Point	suggestion: plant some trees, stone marker
Nevada	13,147	Boundary Peak	½ mile from Cali, connected to

			Montgomery Pk.
New Hampshire	6,288	Mount Washington	4.1-mi. hike, rainy, windy, brrr even in July
New Jersey	1,803	High Point	220-ft. obelisk @ peak, war vet memorial
New Mexico	13,167	Wheeler Peak	crash, real-deal couple, scree slope
New York	5,343	Mount Marcy	ID-ed, posed for pix, signed autographs
North Carolina	6,684	Mount Mitchell	highest Appalachian peak, wild blueberries
North Dakota	3,508	White Butte	shark fin-shaped butte, Baaad lands, sandstone
Ohio	1,549	Campbell Hill	within Bellefontaine city limits, limestone
Oklahoma	4,975	Black Mesa	plateau, lizards run amok, obelisk @ summit
Oregon	11,249	Mount Hood	a.k.a. Wy-east, volcanic, igneous rock
Pennsylvania	3,213	Mount Davis	on ridge, 1 mi. hike, circular stones
Rhode Island	811	Jerimoth Hill	Jerimoth was a rock outcropping, not a bullfrog
South Carolina	3,560	Sassafras Mountain	can't stop saying Sassafras, 300 ft. hike
South Dakota	7,244	Harney Peak	Custer was once here, not sure about Killroy
Tennessee	6,643	Clingman's Dome Mount	Love east of here, metagreywacke
Texas	8,751	Guadalupe Peak	steel pyramid marks summit, no threat to Egypt

Utah	13,534	King's Peak	yet to be climbed
Vermont	4,395	Mount Mansfield	like profile of a human head, hiked to the Nose
Virginia	5,729	Mount Rogers	1.2 mile to Appalachian Trail, rhyolite
Washington	14,417	Mount Rainier	a.k.a. Mother of Waters, heavily glaciated
West Virginia	4,862	Spruce Knob	almost heaven, no need for pepper spray, sandstone
Wisconsin	1,951	Timms Hill	not made of cheese, could use a beer though
Wyoming	13,809	Gannett Peak	yet to be climbed

April's Word/Phrases
List for Hope

(a best of)

(blank) -echoes, -leanings, -speak	a fixer	a smattering
Any circus would be lucky to have you	backsplash	cogitate
death by spreadsheet	comeuppance	dictates of (blank)
echo chamber	dupe	flesh out
Foggy Bottom	nix	jerkwater
heart's circuitry	Puke-ish	makeshift feeling
ice cream intervention	oust	repurposed (blank)
human factors research scientist	ripple with	yanking of (emotion)
level of granularity	pond scum	set of regrets
ungoverned (fill in emotion)	uptick	style points
list of assumptions	impugn	honey trap
swirl of (fill in the blank)	credo	foofaraw
misery index	foist	slippage

Acknowledgments

While writing *LBG*, I immersed myself principally in Jane Austen, John Grisham and Emily Dickinson. Austen penned *Pride & Prejudice, Sense & Sensibility* and five other enduring novels before the age of 41, when she died. Today, her voice still echoes, drumming a cadence that I find myself attempting to emulate (though admittedly in a less verbose, more contemporary form). On the other end of the spectrum, there's Grisham concise. If I could have a cuppa' joe with him, I would. Words would be few, I imagine. None would be wasted. Most of his would be right – a la Emily Dickinson right. While living, despite limited publishing success, Dickinson kept right on writing – 1,775 poems, only 11 published before her passing. Her masterpiece *Hope* now belongs to the ages. *LBG*'s Hope riffed on that poem's "at all" in Chapter 22, ending the novel in tribute.

Five years and three cheap, beat-up, used computers after completing chapter one of *LBG*, I can tell you that seeing a novel through to completion is more difficult than I imagined. Maddening really. It is a rather solitary pursuit, though thankfully not entirely so. Along the way, many offered creative input and healthy critique. Without these contributors, *LBG* would be only a shadow of its final form:

- Angie Menoni Landmesser, who urged me to write LBG, coined the title, loaned Hope her OCD and penned most of the horoscopes

- Editorial input: Laurel Nelson (primary), Karli, Susan and Rebecca

- Publisher: Reagan Rothe & Black Rose Writing for believing

- Outside voices and beta draft readers: Wendy – chapter 1's "bloody stump," "No fun" and the pheromone couple, Jeannie – man-hand expert, Jean – sleepwalking testimonials, Patrice & Sam – barista inspirations, Traci Merekat Gallagher – JELL-O connoisseur who may have "run down that hill" once before (chapter 16), Dawn, the Tiger lady – "fractures" and English soccer chant (chapters 2 & 3), Amy (Marbles) – chapter 4 "signaling" contributor (and for turning the camera back on Hope right away in chapter 6), Half-a-Donut Mary – "world made for couples," Vinny the snake (and her handler Erin), Tina – banterer extraordinaire, Kristen – "terminally single" verbiage, Karen J & Deb – ironing out the wrinkled parts, Carolyn, Rissa (whose name is borrowed by chapter 18's shrink), Gary, Lindsay, Patti, The Michler, Lori, Bogie, Danette, Carla, Carol "the memoir prof," The Ermer, Kalli, Poetess Leslie, Trish, "Trigger," Bill B, Chad R "unforeseen unknowables," Lollypop, Sue, Stella, Jimbo – chapter 5 "world running out of rocks," Kristen, Angi and Kristel – vital shots of feedback, and most importantly, MSF for real-deal inspiration – nothing is this perfect, except this.

- Graphic designers & photographers (for the *LBG* Facebook page): The Danya, Jen L, Bob F and Maureen

- Family love and support: Sam & Maddie Taylor, John, Michael ("needs to shuddap and sing, but mostly just shuddap" – chapter 19) and Barbara & Ed Hughes. ((hugs))

LIKE LBG on FACEBOOK: facebook.com/LoveByGeorge
(memes, quotes, excerpts and updates)

BLACK ROSE writing™

CPSIA information can be obtained
at www.ICGtesting.com
Printed in the USA
BVHW092345270822
645634BV00004B/10